Truth Tales

Truth Tales

Contemporary Stories by Women Writers of India

Edited by Kali for Women

Introduction by Meena Alexander

The Feminist Press at The City University of New York
New York

Published 1990 by The Feminist Press at The City University of New York, 311 East 94 Street, New York, NY 10128

Distributed by The Talman Company, 150 Fifth Avenue, New York, NY 10011

94 93 92 91 90 6 5 4 3 2 1

"The Wet Nurse" by Mahasveta Devi appeared originally in *Ekshon Literary Quarterly* (1976); "The Dolls" by Suniti Aphale in *Surge International;* "Muniyakka" by Lakshmi Kannan in *Commonwealth Quarterly;* "Tiny's Granny" by Ismat Chughtai in *Contemporary Indian Short Stories, 1* (Sahitya Akademi, 1959); and "Midnight Soldiers" by Vishwapriya Iyengar in *Imprint* (March 1986).

Library of Congress Cataloging-in-Publication Data

Truth tales : contemporary stories by women writers of India / edited
  by Kali for Woman ; introduction by Meena Alexander.
    p.   cm.
  Short stories, six of them translated from Indian languages.
    Contents: The wet nurse / Mahasveta Devi — Smoke / Ila Mehta —
The dolls / Suniti Aphale — Tragedy, in a minor key / Mrinal Pande
—Muniyakka / Lakshmi Kannan — Tiny's granny / Ismat Chughtai —
Midnight soldiers / Vishwapriya Iyengar.
    ISBN 1-55861-011-1. — ISBN 1-55861-012-X (pbk.)
    1. Short stories, Indic—Translations into English.   2. Short
stories, English—Translations from foreign languages.   3. Short
stories, Indic—Women authors.   4. Indic fiction—20th century.
PK5461.T78   1990
891'.4—dc20   89-78155
                                                                  CIP

Cover art by Chandralekha, Skills, Madras, India

Cover design by Lucinda Geist

Text design by Paula Martinac

Printed in the United States of America on pH-neutral paper by
McNaughton & Gunn, Inc.

This publication is made possible, in part, by public funds from the
New York State Council on the Arts and the National Endowment for
the Arts. The Feminist Press is also grateful to Karen Twitchell for her
generosity.

Contents

Preface

Many years ago when the idea of Kali for Women first came to mind, a book such as this was among the first we planned. The idea grew out of the conviction that there existed, outside the framework of Indo-Anglian writing (which had come to be seen as modern Indian writing), a wealth of literature in the regional languages that represented some of the most dynamic trends in Indian writing, that had had little exposure beyond its region. The nationalist movement for independence in the early part of this century, more recent political developments, the growth of leftist and women's movements, and the many cultures and literary traditions of this country all had impinged in some way on creativity and writing.

For us it became important to ask how these experiences had touched upon women's writing on the whole. Did this writing address itself to certain questions? How did the women themselves see such writing? Was it marginal or central to their lives? What was the relationship between such writing and the political involvement of the writers? Can one detect any regionality in them? What are their concerns, and what is the creative energy at work? We felt that putting together such a volume was one way of trying to find answers to these questions.

The process of locating, identifying, and translating the kind of fiction that we thought existed was not an easy one. Little was available by way of information. Occasionally, stray

stories appeared in magazines and newspapers. Translations
that remained faithful to the spirit of the original were difficult
to find, authors sometimes untraceable. Unfamiliarity with the
language or the region proved a barrier. Gradually, however,
through personal contact, word of mouth and authors putting
us in touch with others, we managed to garner a set of stories
that together create a rich mosaic of Indian life.

The selection presented here is far from being either complete or definitive, and often the stories determinedly elude
categories and questions. The aim behind such a volume, however, is not to be representative, but to reflect some of the
richness of writing that is available today. The seven stories
selected are from seven major languages—Bengali, Gujarati,
Marathi, Hindi, Urdu, Tamil and English—each with a vigorous
literary tradition, and each representing seven distinct sensibilities. Geographically, they are spread across the subcontinent in easily recognizable locations (rural, urban, small town,
cosmopolitan) and easily identifiable situations. Each story is,
nevertheless, strongly individual; many reflect a particular regional consciousness arching out into the commonality of
women's experiences. Rooted in a particular context, growing
out of that idiom, written with a sensibility that belongs, a
sensitivity that is deeply sympathetic, these stories cull the
essence of women's experiences: the power, the passion, the
pain, the hopelessness, the fury, the joy. The predicaments
these women find themselves in are not untypical: It is their
individual responses to them that define the women, their
social milieu, and its mores.

The spectrum of talent here is as wide as the age span of the
writers. The older among them have lived through—at times
actively participated in—national liberation struggles, have been
part of a literary renaissance that was especially evident in
western and eastern India, and continue to be politically active
today. Others, younger perhaps, come with a finely tuned
consciousness born of their experience with post-independence

leftist and women's movements. Still others see themselves as writers first and last, albeit with their fingers on the pulse of women's being. Together, through the texture of their stories and the tone and timbre of their voices, all of them communicate the vibrancy of women's writing today.

Meena Alexander ━━

Introduction

In contemporary India, where ancient cultures, hierarchical and exclusive, exist in a tension with a rapidly changing
society, the place prescribed for women becomes a fault line, a
site of potential rupture. As such it bears revolutionary potential. India, which gained its independence in 1947, is the world's
largest democracy and has one of the strongest feminist movements in the Third World. Women's activism coheres frequently
around life and death issues including basic health care and safe
contraception (there have been campaigns against dangerous
drugs dumped by Western pharmaceutical companies in India),
subsistence wages for women, day care centers for women
laborers on building sites—so infants will not be maimed by
falling rocks or debris—as well as protests and legal action
against more incendiary issues: gang rape of women in police
stations, the revival of sati (the ritual immolation of widows),
and dowry deaths.

Truth Tales, a collection of short stories by Indian women
translated from six languages, comes from this world. The ages
of the writers span the decades of modern India: the oldest was
born in 1915, the youngest in 1958. There is an ancient tradition
of women's writing in India, at least two thousand years old,
and each of these stories draws on a different linguistic tradition: Bengali, Gujarati, Marathi, Hindi, Tamil, Urdu, and English—the last, one of the languages of postcolonial India.[1]

Obviously there is no attempt at being comprehensive. Numerous languages with major literary traditions have no say here. But the purpose of this little collection as the Preface indicates is to give the general reader a sense of the intensity of contemporary Indian women's short fiction.

In this book, we read in turn about a wet nurse, a woman doctor, a dollmaker, a college student, a cleaning woman, a vagrant, and a fisherwoman. The protagonists come from varying castes and classes of Indian society. While no one is wealthy, several are comfortably off. But there is also subsistence-level poverty depicted here, the desperate marginality of a female existence where each day's labor must stretch for the evening's food. Whether these women live in solitude, in extended families, or in nuclear families, we see clearly how female labor stitches the world together. And in choosing to speak from within woman's condition, these female voices have already decolonized themselves. Nor are they haunted by a gaze that makes them Other, in the Western use of the term. Whatever the actual and often desperate marginality of their lot, there is a fierce attachment to the material conditions of life, and the women in these fictive worlds speak for themselves.

Where the ritual feminine marks out the limits of their possibilities the women struggle on. Often there is no clear resolution in sight. In the haunting story "Smoke" by Ila Mehta, a young woman doctor drives her car to the clinic and conducts her professional business, but at home lives in perpetual fear that her mother-in-law will catch her smoking. Shubha's addiction to cigarettes, an index of the nervous distress that consumes her, is part and parcel of her life as a young widow. Her husband of four months was killed in a car crash. His life has ended but in accordance with custom she is still bound to him. Her mother-in-law keeps watch over the proprieties. But for Shubha the daily tasks of veneration, lighting incense sticks, placing fresh garlands of flowers around the dead man's photograph, have less and less meaning. She is trapped. In her time widow remarriage is not yet common practice. Can she move forward?

In India, the ritually prescribed status of the feminine is still crucial to woman's grasp of herself. Often it maps out the world, defines what is sanctioned as possible. Veneration of the maternal, of the powers of nurturing and mothering are inscribed in the tradition. While there are godesses in the cultures of Hinduism blessed with awesome powers, the fabric of day-to-day society, the lines of descent, the mechanics of public power, are most often patriarchal in fact and intent. Brought up to believe in arranged marriage, tutored to the veneration of the mother-in-law in whom great power is vested, the young woman finds herself doubly displaced by marriage. She is cut off from her maternal home, and she must "reeducate" herself to the tasks and duties of her husband's family. There is a whole tradition of poignant folk songs in India, sung by the mother and daughter when they part. The girl will only return to her parents' home sporadically. The birth of a child is a time to return. If the child is male, the marriage is thought to be fulfilled.

Female sexuality, of course, must be carefully controlled. Marriage is permitted only within the circle of prescribed families, compatible according to genealogy and background. In at least two of the stories here, "The Dolls" and "Tragedy in a Minor Key," there are allusions to how lovers may not marry because of a discrepancy in their castes. But this does not stop up desire. It finds other channels.

Indeed the richness of Indian society lies in the multitude of fluid selves that are possible to a person. The self is not cut up into conflicting categories: woman who is mother/worker/wife/writer; woman who juggles many lives. Rather in a tradition that defines the "self" as communal, as intrinsically relational, a multitude of lives are possible, and the possibilities can stretch both the female imagination and the social fabric in which it is wrapped. In the finely wrought "Dolls" the protagonist, an artist figure, a dollmaker, still loves the man she is not permitted to marry. When he dies, she continues to provide for his son and widow. The story turns around her sense of being exploited—she needs terribly to be needed—and how that threatens her passionate creativity. A fiercely independent woman, Shakun lives in a world that is swiftly changing. A merchant from Bombay comes to buy her dolls to sell them to foreign tourists for large sums of money. He is of a certain age, newly divorced. Might he desire her? The thought attracts and worries her.

But to return to the scenario I outlined earlier—the young woman, compliant, faithful, drawn into an arranged marriage and life within the extended family where the mother-in-law rules—it is surely significant that not one of the stories sticks to this script. The traditional feminine models of Sita and Savitri (Sita the pure, chaste wife of Lord Rama; Savitri whose devotion to her husband Satyavan led her into the realms of death), mythic figures of shining spousal faith, are never followed through here. For this is female writing, fierce, insurgent. The words often spill from an excess that the bodily being cannot herself wholly grasp. They fracture established patterns, point out the necessity of difference. What is female power here? What is the bodily truth of women? The questions, though seemingly general, are concentrated in intent, bound up with the links between femininity and power, implicating the larger issues of political will.

A slight detour can help us explore the tension between femininity and female power.[2] In 1913, Rabindranath Tagore, the great Bengali poet, composed a play based on an episode in the Hindu epic *The Mahabharata*. He titled the play *Chitra*, after its female protagonist. Young Princess Chitra, only child of the King of Manipur, is dressed in masculine garb and reared to be a warrior. She is strong limbed, and quite fearless. She is able to defend the boundaries of the kingdom. But desire dissolves her world. She falls in love with Arjuna and her pride, her fear-lessness vanish. The stereotypical language of love intrudes:

she would be anything to be near him, even a clod of clay under his feet. In despair she turns to Madana, the God of Love. She wants Arjuna to desire her. Her need to be wanted bends her to the requirements of femininity. Female power must be cast aside. Chitra clothes herself in silks and jewels: "For the first time in my life I felt myself a woman, and knew that a man was before me." But her body is too plain to attract Arjuna. She pleads with Madana for beauty sufficient to draw Arjuna to her. She must exist in his desire, her body molded by Arjuna's need.

But after a night of lovemaking, the new beautiful Princess Chitra wakes up weeping: "Heaven came so close to my hand . . . but when I woke in the morning from my dream I found that my body had become my own rival." Her poignant phrase "I found that my body had become my own rival" could only come from the mouth of a being taught to measure her own value through the eyes of another, alienated from her own bodily being.

The iconic feminine that Chitra has so painfully and assiduously sought—what, paradoxically, her father the king had shielded her from—now destroys her need for truth and self-respect. There is a humiliation in being desired for what one is not. The feminine consciousness is painfully divided. Having given up power and virility for femininity, a body that Arjuna could desire, Princess Chitra despises herself. She is consumed by a sense of unreality. Her lovely limbs, the laughter, the grace that had so attracted Arjuna all seem mere simulacra. The cleft between "woman's beauty" and "man's strength" is highlighted, then miraculously resolved, as Chitra returns to her old, well-worn form assuring Arjuna that when in the fullness of time she bears him a son, he will truly know her. Only then will the brave, daring, yet finally feminine Chitra fulfill herself. As one reads the last words of the play, the heroine defining herself through the unborn son she bears within her, perfect semblance of the father, one realizes something of the force of the iconic feminine that the female imagination has had to confront: "If your babe, whom I am nourishing in my womb be born a son, I shall teach him to be a second Arjuna, and send him to you when the time comes, and then at last you will truly know me."[3]

Tagore's sensitivity to Chitra's lot is underwritten, however, by the ideology he questions but ultimately accepts: one that decrees that femininity must exist as the complement to masculine power, not as its subversive supplement, an excess that would undermine the boundaries of gender. In the resolution of the play, Arjuna's image of Chitra riding again on a white horse, spear in hand and victorious, is predicated on her potential as a bearer of sons. Her labor, her bodily activity, must ultimately be validated not by what she is, powerful and active, but through her reproductive powers that will perpetuate the male lineage. The preface, setting out the Mahabharata story, reminds us that Chitra's birth as a woman was an aberration. In a long line of heirs to the kingdom, she was the first to have been born female. She was taught to be male but succumbed in the end to desire, the mark of her femaleness. Value is recuperated through her maternity, her ability to bear a son.

In "The Wet Nurse," the little masterpiece with which this collection opens, the icons of femininity and maternity are picked up and smashed. Jashoda's body is not her rival. Her rival is the life she has been given. Her breasts, with their miraculous supply of milk permit her to earn a living and feed her own family. But in multiple senses she is in bonded labor. While the daughters-in-law of the wealthy Halder family maintain their bosoms, Jashoda—named after the mother of Lord Krishna, the beloved dark lord of salvation and erotic play— bears child after child, nurses one Halder grandchild after another. Finally, her breasts ulcerated, burning with a thousand sores, she finds herself unwanted and outcast. The doctor who sees her, a modern man, is stunned that one woman could have nursed fifty mouths. Abandoned by the Halders whose offspring she has nursed for so many years, neglected by her crippled husband, ignored by her sons, Jashoda seizes at the humbug surrounding maternity: "Motherhood is a terrible addiction; once you are hooked it is difficult to withdraw even after the milk has run dry" (49).

Mahasveta Devi, one of India's major writers has long been a political activist. She has dedicated herself to working with the underprivileged, including the tribals who have suffered indignity and oppression at the hands of the government. Her political understanding of the social basis of inequity, her refusal of easy ideologies—whether religious or familial—enable her to expose the terror at the heart of Jashoda's condition. While Mahasveta's wit and humor irradiate the narrative voice and her political analysis prevents the vision from lapsing into the tragic, there is nothing consoling about what happens to Jashoda the wet nurse. Sucked dry, she becomes outcaste: "One had to be a Jashoda to nurse the world. One also had to die alone, friendless . . . Jashoda's death was god's death. In this world . . . when a person takes on godhood . . . he is rejected by everyone and is left to die alone" (61–62).

Femininity is power, exploited power. The female body maintains the world. It produces labor, it reproduces. It peoples the continent. It is used up and cast out. In a culture hung up on purity and pollution, dominated by the social horror of untouchability, the female body crosses all barriers. It is mobile, rich, metamorphic. In Mahasveta's imagination unclouded by the ideologies of consolation, the used up female body becomes mere waste to be burned. Yet it is simultaneously what was construed as god. Old Halder, who made his money during the British regime, and his son who drives a Studebaker and runs over poor Kangalicharan's feet, inadvertently sending Jashoda in search of a livelihood, are both intrinsic to a society that can venerate the Brahmin whose legs were cut off and destroy him in poverty. The lines of caste and class do not intersect, nor do the lines of necessity and greed. The struggling priest and guide of the temple of Simhavahini can turn the goddess's face one way or the other to serve his interests; Jashoda, dependent on her milk for sustenance, tugged by dreams of social ease, washing her breasts with fine soaps, will sublimate into the goddess Simhavahini, she who once appeared in Jashoda's vision in the form of a midwife, bag in hand. The lure of fate, the noose of desire, the base constructions of religion, are all highlighted by Mahasveta Devi. Time and again in her writings the female body becomes the site of a truly subversive reckoning of reality.[4]

Indeed reality, the skin of things as they are, must be torn apart in the interests of a better order. And women's writing plays its part in the struggle. There is a strong tradition of women's writing in India that stands askew from the status quo and its hierarchical, caste-ridden orderings: works as various as the songs of Mirabai (c.1498–1565), a woman poet of the Bhakti movement who rejoices in disruptive, ecstatic love of Lord Krishna; or the outraged feminist fictions of the Malayalam novelist Lalithambika Antherjanam (1909–1987). In her celebrated novel *Agnisakshi (Trial by Fire)*, Antherjanam tells of the life of Tethi, an intelligent young woman married into a strict Namboodiri household and condemned to live in accordance with traditional ritualistic demands.[5] Tethi's frustration grows unbearable. Responding to Gandhi's call for women satyagrahis, activists to follow his path of nonviolent civil disobedience, she bursts free. The narrative framework is crucial. Tethi's swiftly changing, irretrievably unstable life is recounted: the names she uses and casts aside, the rage that drives her. The consciousness that spells all this out is that of her sister-in-law Thankam. Where strict Namboodiri practice is concerned Thankam, born of a Nair mother, is an untouchable. Her ritual status as outcaste sharpens the feminist insight, making up the perfect frame for a life in revolt.

The capacity for female revolt is clearly seen in the last story of the collection, "Midnight's Soliders" by Vishwapriya Iyengar, a tale set in an impoverished Catholic community on the coast of Kerala. The protagonist, Matilda, is a lonely independent woman. With her dwindling sum of money—her husband has taken to drink, her little children are sick, the older boy afflicted with an incurable kidney disease—she must purchase fish and carry her catch into the market place to sell, often walking fifteen miles each way. Her livelihood, like that of the other fisherfolk is endangered by modern trawlers initially introduced by the Norwegian fisheries, mechanized vessels that indiscriminately drag in young fish and eggs, destroying the future harvests.

The intersecting claims of maternity and livelihood provide the explosive tension. With its socialist tradition, Kerala has a well-developed program of contraception for women. Matilda, visited by a social worker who shows her photos of two well-groomed children in velvet chairs, their wealthy parents taking tea, is enticed. She is seduced by the fantasy of an easy life: "She went to the big hospital in Trivandrum . . . It wasn't an operation, it was a prayer, a dream of satin ribbons, and of drinking tea together" (168). Matilda has her operation and the irreversible nature of the procedure is strongly implied. But in a culture of poverty, early sicknesses may well prove fatal: the baby Yetta has dysentery. Laid in a cradle of sand while her mother stalks the market roads at night to sell her big fish, the infant weakens and dies. Coming upon the dead body of her child, Matilda races out of her hut, fish in one hand, the wasted body of her child in the other. As she screams, fisherwomen rush toward her, then stand utterly still as the ocean—Kaddallamma, Mother Sea—breaks itself against the southern coast. Though there are times when the intensity seems forced, the story coheres into a powerful piece. In a world of underdevelopment, the attempts at modernization (trawlers, the means of contraception) can be treacherous. The women, those who hold the world together with their labor, also bear the brunt of despair: "a long line of midnight soldiers . . . Where would they burn this fire that always burnt them?" (172).

Women know the edges of chaos so intensely because it is our task to hold the world together, maintain the fabric of daily life. The preservation of the human world in its most intimate shape—the spaces of domesticity—is necessarily charged. In

Suniti Aphale's moving story "The Dolls" we are given a subtle, and quite unusual, reading of female labor and care. Shakun, who has never married, is able to live an independent life because of her gift for making life-like dolls. As mentioned earlier, the dolls are sold through a middleman in Bombay. In her art Shakun is able to create an elegant economy of gesture, a beauty and poise sadly lacking in her life. Obsessed by her craft—the dolls she confesses "grab you round the throat like ghosts" (72)—she lives alone but spends a great deal of energy and money attending to the needs of Nirupama. Kanti, the man Shakun loved and Nirupama married is dead now, and Nirupama has remarried, but the bonds of dependency, first encouraged by Shakun in her guilt, are now exploited by the self-serving Nirupama. Shakun pays for the college education of her dead lover's son; she helps out Ramnik the widower and his two children; lacking blood relatives she makes up a family for herself.

Time and again Shakun's sexuality surfaces and then is thrust aside as her fears follow. Why did Ramnik the merchant marry Nirupama rather than her? Was Shakun too attractive, too strong? Does Kishorebai the Bombay middleman really want her? Or does he, like everyone else, only take her for granted? The delicate bodies of her dolls cannot quite console her. In her anger, she refuses Kishorebhai the dolls he has come for, but then suddenly relents. Her need is too fierce: "She wanted him to go on depending on her . . . She wanted that very much . . . to help others had been the mainstay of her life" (95).

It is no accident that the elaborate dance that Shakun represents through her dolls, and which effectively torments her, is the gharba, a riotous celebration of fecundity. The closure of the story, reached after a passage of sexual despair and exhaustion, is instructive. The artist persists. Making dolls up from wax and silk and clay, she permits herself to live on. Her discipline is essential to survival: "She went on sewing the folds without bothering whether the needle would hurt her" (96).

Each of these stories articulates a form of survival. In Mrinal Pande's "Tragedy in a Minor Key" the narrator is a young college student stifled by her family life. The voice cascades on in an ever so slight craziness through the lethargy and boredom of a middle-class world where a young woman's horizon can only be marriage, arranged according to custom and the horoscope. In such a world a middle-aged Malini Mausi may not survive her youth and beauty with innocence intact: "All her pronouncements swung between an acute hatred of her femininity and a black self-pity" (103). Though her readings of Perry Mason mysteries and Mills and Boon pulp romances can hardly save her, the narrator, blessed with a vivid realism and a self-deprecating humor survives moments that carry her to the brink of hysteria.

Old age has its own compulsions. In "Tiny's Granny" the distinguished fiction writer Ismat Chughtai presents the world of an old vagrant, nameless except for a tag signaling her bond to familial others. She is named and renamed: "Baftan's kid," "Bashirah's daughter-in-law," "Bismillah's mother," and finally "Tiny's granny." The last name sticks with her till death. While the lack of a name of her own testifies to her marginality, we recall that such bonds with familial others are precisely what the dollmaker Shakun lacks. Of the old woman Chughtai writes: "God knows what her real name was. No one had ever called her by it" (146). Working at odd jobs for a pittance, gossiping, carrying tales back and forth, filching odd bits of food and drink, Tiny's granny survives. As best she can she shields the young child. But at the age of nine poor Tiny is raped by the Deputy Sahib and no one dares raise a protest. The child shivers and hides away, then seems to recover. But in reality she turns brazen, promiscuous, robbed of her innocence. When she disappears from the town the old grandmother mourns her death. Her distress culminates when a pillow she prizes is pinched by competitors for scraps of discarded food, the neighborhood monkeys. Out of the torn pillow spill momentos Tiny's granny has stolen, then hoarded for years: "Shabban's quilted jacket . . . Bannu the water carrier's waistcloth . . . Hasina's bodice . . ." (155). The list goes on and on. It includes beads and prayer boards, dried navel strings and turmeric in a sachet: the essence of the world hoarded up to keep her going. The towns-people raise a hue and cry. Grief stricken, the old granny rocks all night on her haunches, back and forth. In the morning she is discovered stone dead, flies crawling in the corners of her eyes. Body too stiff to be laid out, she is shrouded as she is; buried in her tatters.

In Ismat Chughtai's writing, as in the work of Mahasveta Devi, there is a sense of a whole universe of thought and feeling compressed into the bounds of the short story: a complex, vibrant whole. In "Tiny's Granny," a description of the uses to which the burqua can be put merit notice: a marvelous celebration of the tactics of survival, of life at the edge. The seams in the yards of cloth that compose the burqua, complete with cap and veil that should shield her modesty as befits a Muslim woman, have long since fallen apart. Now the remnants, cap and back-cloth, are lovingly patched with oddments and serve Tiny's granny as sleeping bag and bedclothes, pillow, towel, prayer mat, even a shield against snarling dogs.

In the powerful yet delicately constructed "Muniyakka" by poet Lakshmi Kannan—who writes both in Tamil and English—we have an old woman, Muniyakka, given to soliloquies. The children dub her "Walkie-Talkie" for her habit of muttering to herself. Another old woman at the edge of society, another improvized existence. But, unlike the fierce attachment to the world seen in "Tiny's Granny," here the passions of want, need, and attachment are swept aside in the internal movements of the mind. The edge of chaos is ontological. The pattern is drawn from the nirguna mode of devotion. Traditional Hinduism provides two, at times entwined, modes of access to divinity. The mode of saguna implies a devotion filled with qualities: the human forms and attachments that celebrate the world. Lord Krishna, whose form so entices the dollmaker Shakun and sends her fingers twitching, is perhaps the most beloved of these divine incarnations. The way of nirguna (literally "without qualities" or "shorn of substance") leads to an emptying of the mind, a shearing away of the phenomenal, the already given world. It is here that the old Muniyakka leads us. After the labor of her day, washing vessels in houses, swabbing floors, cleaning the temple stones, her mind moves freely. The burdens slip off: "In that still moment, she felt quite empty. Her mind was swept clean like the interior of the hut, purged of all disturbing thoughts and stilled to a mute point" (141). The spiritual poise flickers and vanishes. It is necessarily brief. Whether she is washing the temple stones carved in the ritual image of the cobra, stained with lines of kumkum, turmeric, and sandal paste, splattered with berries—old now, feeling the neglect of her sons, she has little patience for the women who crowd here praying for the boon of fertility—or whether she is preparing the simple sraddha, death ceremonies for her husband, Bairappa, complete with a freshly cooked meal on a banana leaf, true meaning for Muniyakka lies elsewhere. As a storm gathers and branches sway, she feels her mind dancing with the fury of Kali, the great goddess of destruction. The world must be cleansed, made up again. The mind touches its own limits:

> Who's a devil? And who's not a devil?
> Who am I? (145).

The great waves of destruction are part of the cycle of things. All names and stations are lost as the female voice glimpses the nothingness that underwrites material existence.

Notes

1. In 1990 and 1991 The Feminist Press will publish a two-volume anthology of over two thousand years of writings by Indian women. The volumes include songs, devotionals, protest literature, as well as fiction, poetry, and autobiography.

2. For a further analysis see Meena Alexander, "Outcaste Power: Ritual Displacement and Virile Maternity in Indian Women Writers," in *Economic and Political Weekly,* vol. XXIV, no. 7 (February 18, 1989),

originally presented as the Francis Wayland Collegium Lecture, Brown University, October 1987.

3. Rabindranath Tagore, *Chitra, A Play in One Act* (Madras: Macmillan Publishers, 1985), pp. 6, 26, 55, 66–67.

4. For a variant translation as well as an acute political and literary analysis of this story (the title is rendered as "Breast-Giver"), see Gayatri Chakravorty Spivak *In Other Worlds, Essays in Cultural Politics* (New York and London: Routledge, 1988). Spivak's translation preserves in italicized form the English words Mahasveta Devi has scattered through her text. For instance, just picking the first three: "drill," "professional mother," and "amateur." The ironic function of these words would work well for a Bengali audience. Spivak aptly reads it as "a parable of India after decolonization" (*In Other Worlds*, 244).

5. Lalithambika Antherjanam, *Agnisakshi*, trans. Vasanthi Sankaranaragan (Trichur, India: Kerala Sahitya Akademi, 1980).

Mahasveta Devi ▰ *(Bengali)*

The Wet Nurse

My aunt who lived in the thicket
My aunt who lived far away,
My aunt never called me fondly
To give me peppermints or candy.

*J*ashoda cannot remember whether her own aunt treated her as badly as the one in the children's rhyme, or looked after her well. More likely, right from her birth she has been just Kangalicharan's wife and the mother of twenty children, if you count both the living and the dead. She cannot remember a time when she was not carrying a child in her womb or when she was free from spells of morning sickness. Nor can she recall the darkness of a single night, intensified by the light of the small oil lamp, when Kangalicharan's body did not bore into her like a geologist's drill.

Jashoda never had the time to decide whether she could or couldn't tolerate motherhood. Interminable motherhood was the only way she could keep her large family alive. She was a professional mother; it was her career. She was not an amateur in the game like the women in the bhadralog, babu households. After all, this world is the monopoly of professionals. The city has no time for amateur beggars, pickpockets, or whores; even the street dogs and crows hanging around trash cans, tempted by the garbage, will not yield an inch of their territory to an amateur newcomer. And so, perforce, Jashoda took up motherhood as a profession.

The responsibility for this, of course, lay with the Studebaker that belonged to the new son-in-law of the Halder household, and with Halderbabu's youngest son's sudden desire to drive a car in the middle of the day. The suddenness of the desire was nothing new: the boy was driven by all kinds of unexpected whims and physical impulses which would not let him rest until satisfied. Funnily enough, these strange desires surfaced in the noontime solitude to drive him relentlessly on, like the slave of a caliph of Baghdad. Still, up to now Jashoda's taking to motherhood as a career was not in any way connected with what the young fellow did as a result of his afternoon vagaries.

For example, one day, driven by lust, he assaulted the family cook. She was lethargic after a heavy meal of rice, fish head (slyly hidden from her mistress's hawk eyes), and some delicious greens specially cooked, so she relaxed, lay back, and said, "Do what you like." At last the Baghdadi spirit released him from its grip and the boy shed tears of remorse, pleading with the cook, "Don't tell anyone, mashi." The cook shrugged off the whole incident, said, "What is there to say about it?" and promptly went to sleep.

She would never have disclosed the story to anyone because she was quite pleased that her body had attracted the young man. But the guilty tend to become excessively sensitive; seeing extra large helpings of fish and other goodies on his plate, the boy became alarmed. He felt that he would be in the dock if the cook decided to expose him. So one afternoon, driven by his Baghdadi djinn, he stole his mother's ring and hid it inside the cook's pillowcase. He then raised a hue and cry, leading to her dismissal.

Another afternoon he stole his father's radio and sold it. It was difficult for his parents to see the link between the boy's capricious behavior and the afternoon siesta, because in keeping with the tradition of the Harishal Halders, the father created his children only in the depth of the night, after duly consulting the almanac. (In fact, once you cross the gate you find that the household is still in the grip of the sixteenth century, and that almanacs guide the days of cohabitation with one's wife.) But these are peripheral matters, mere bye-lanes to the real destination, which is Jashoda's story.

Kangalicharan worked in a sweet shop. He made sweets for those Brahmin pilgrims to the temple of Simhavahini (the Lion Goddess) who are proud of their caste and still observe the taboos regarding food. He would fry puris in keeping with the shop advertisement: "Puris and curry prepared by a good Brahmin." In the process, he would filch a bit of flour or this and that to help in the smooth running of his own household. One afternoon Kangalicharan was returning home after handing over charge of the shop to the owner. Tucked away in the folds of his dhoti were a few samosas and jalebis which he had pinched from the shop. (Returning home at midday is part of his daily routine; he and his wife Jashoda eat their daily lunch of rice at that time. His hunger appeased, he would be overcome by filial emotion towards Jashoda and fondle her full breasts a little before falling off to sleep.) On that particular afternoon Kangalicharan was returning home, as was his wont, thinking of the pleasures that awaited him at home, particularly Jashoda's breasts. The thought filled him with ecstasy. At this moment of anticipated heavenly joy, the youngest Halder son in the Studebaker screeched to a halt, missing Kangalicharan by the skin of his teeth, but not quite able to save his feet. Both these were mangled beyond repair.

Crowds gathered in a trice. Nabin Panda shouted threateningly: "We would have shed blood if the accident had happened anywhere other than in front of the Halder home!" Nabin is a priest and a guide in the temple of the Goddess, who is a direct manifestation of Shakti, and so it is but natural that in the hot afternoon sun his temper took an upward swing. His bellowing succeeded in bringing everyone out of the Halder home.

Old man Halder started thrashing his son and screaming at him, "You ass, you blockhead, do you want to kill a Brahmin?" The son-in-law, seeing his Studebaker just a little damaged, heaved a sigh of relief and proceeded to prove what a vastly superior human being he was compared to his in-laws, who may have amassed money but were totally devoid of any cultural refinement whatsoever. In a voice as fine as the finest cambric, he asked delicately: "Will you let the man die? Won't you take him to the hospital?"

Kangali's employer was also in the crowd. Seeing the scattered samosas and jalebis, he was about to say: "Shame on you Kangali that you should do this!" But he changed his mind and said guardedly, "You do that, dada." The son-in-law and Halder senior promptly took Kangalicharan to the hospital.

Old Halder felt genuinely sorry. During the Second World War he had assisted the antifascist war of the Allies by buying and selling scrap iron. Kangalicharan was then only in his teens. Respect for Brahmins was ingrained in him and he would start the day by touching a Brahmin's feet. If Chatterjee Babu was not available then he would take a grain of dust from Kangalicharan's cracked soles, Kangalicharan who was young enough to be his son. On festivals and special religious occasions, Kangalicharan and Jashoda came to the house, and when the daughters-in-law became pregnant, a sari and sindur would be sent to Jashoda.

Old Halder brought himself back to the present, consoling Kangali. "Do not worry, my son. As long as I am there I will not let you suffer." Even as he said this, the thought that Kangali's feet had turned into mincemeat flitted through his mind and he realized that when he needed them, Kangali's feet would not be there for him to touch. Regret welled up within him and he cried, "What did the son of a bitch do?" His eyes filled with tears. He appealed to the doctors at the hospital: "Do everything possible for him. Don't worry about money."

But the doctors could not return the soles of his feet to

Kangali. He returned home a defective Brahmin. Old Halder ordered a pair of crutches for him. The day Kangali returned home armed with his crutches, he learned that Jashoda had received a food parcel every day from the Halder household in his absence.

Nabin Panda was third in the line of temple priests. He was entitled to less than one-sixth from the sale of temple prasad, and the constant, nagging unhappiness of this made him feel like a worm. After seeing a film on Ramakrishna, he was inspired by the saint's manner and started addressing the deity with great familiarity. He also started getting sozzled on ritual spirit in the good old tradition of Shakti worship.

He now informed Kangali, "I offered flowers to my beti for your welfare. And the pagli said to me that in Kangali's house there is an incarnation of mine. It will be only because of her that Kangali will return home safe and sound."

Wanting to recount this conversation to Jashoda, Kangali scolded her suspiciously, "So this is what you were doing when I was absent? Carrying on with that rascal Nabin?" Jashoda clasped the mistrusting head between the two hemispheres of her body and assured him, "Every night two maidservants from Halderbabu's place came and slept here in order to guard me. Why should I encourage that crook Nabin? Am I not your chaste wife?"

In fact, even when Kangali went to visit the Halder household, he had proof of the fiery glow of his wife's shining chastity. Jashoda threw herself at the feet of gods and godmen, she performed all kinds of rituals and sat in front of Simhavahini's temple without food and water till the Great Mother appeared to her in a dream in the form of a midwife, complete with a midwife's bag under her arm, and told her, "Do not worry. Your husband will come back."

Hearing all this, Kangali was overwhelmed. Old Halder explained to him, "Would you believe it, Kangali, these cynics say that if Simhavahini had to appear, why would she do so in the guise of a midwife? I reasoned with them: as a mother she conceives and creates and as a midwife she brings children into the world and looks after them."

After all this, Kangali ventured to speak to Halderbabu, "Babu, how can I work any longer in the sweet shop? How will I stir with a ladle when I can only stand supported by a crutch under my arm? To me you are like a god. You are providing for so many people in so many ways. Please also provide me with some work. I do not want to presume on your goodness and beg."

Halderbabu answered, "Of course, Kangali, I have thought of a place for you. I will make a little shop for you in my front verandah. You can sell puffed rice, popped rice, candy sugar and dry foodstuff. Mother Simhavahini is right in front of us, the pilgrims come and go, so you won't lack customers. Just now there is a wedding in the house, so there will be a little delay in starting the shop. It is my seventh brat's marriage. So till that time a hamper of food will be sent to your house everyday."

Hearing this, Kangali's feelings soared like the joyous mating flight of ants signalling the coming of the rains. Going back home, he told Jashoda, "Do you remember that saying of Kalidas, 'You can have it because it is not there; if it was there, then could you have it?' This is true of our luck. Halderbabu has said that after his son's wedding is over, he will start a shop for me, covering a portion of his front verandah. Till that time he will send us food parcels. If my shanks were there would all these good things have happened? It is all the Great Mother's will."

Clattering about on his crutches, Kangali spread the good tidings of his changing fortune to all and sundry. As a result, his former employer, Nabin Panda, Kesho Mahanti who ran a flower shop, and Ulhas, the regular drummer in the temple, all acknowledged: "What a miracle! You can't dismiss everything as Kaliyug. This after all is the Great Mother's realm. Here good deeds and virtue shall reign. Evil will be destroyed. Otherwise, why should Kangali lose his legs? Or, for that matter, why on earth should old Halder, fearing the curse of a Brahmin, take all this trouble? And the most important question is why should Mother appear as a midwife in Jashoda's dreams? It is all her will."

Everyone was amazed that the Goddess Simhavahini, whose discovery and setting up in a temple was the result of a dream some hundred and fifty years ago, should manifest herself around Kangalicharan Patitunda in the fifth decade of this century. After all, old Halderbabu's change of heart was also the Mother's will.

It was well known that Halderbabu was quite selective about distributing his largesse. He was a citizen of free India, where all men were considered equal, where there is supposed to be no distinction between the states, language groups, castes, communities and classes of people. But he had made his pile during the British regime when divide and rule was the policy. That was when his mentality was molded. As a result he did not trust Punjabis-Oriyas-Biharis-Gujaratis-Marathis-Muslims. His heart, well-ensconced in its layer of fat under a size 42 Gopal vest, did not itch with charity when he saw a Bihari child in distress or a starving Oriya beggar.

He was the patriotic son of Harishal, now in Bangladesh, so that even when he saw the common housefly of West Bengal, he would exclaim: "Ah! The flies at home were so fat and healthy. Here in this godforsaken place everything is so scrawny!" No wonder the hangers-on in and around the temple were astonished to see that same Halder drip with mercy over Kangalicharan who very much belonged to the Gangetic delta.

People could not stop talking about it. Halderbabu was such a chauvinist that when his nephews and grandchildren were studying the lives of the great sons of our motherland, he used to remark to his employees, "Huh! Why do they teach them the lives of the Jessore-born, Dacca-born, Mymensingh-born great men? They should be taught the strength of the men of Harishal. The men of Harishal are made of the bones of Dadhichi. In times to come it will be revealed that the Vedas and the Upanishads were written by the Harishals. You will see."

His underlings now told him, in a ridiculous mixture of Bengali and English, "Sir you have had a change of heart. Otherwise how can you harbor so much kindness for a West Bengali? You will see, Sir, God must have some purpose behind this." The boss was overjoyed to hear this and said, smiling broadly, "A Brahmin is a Brahmin. There are no distinctions of West Bengal and East Bengal as far as a Brahmin is concerned. Even when he is shitting, if you were to see the sacred thread, you would have to pay your respects." He laughed loudly at his own joke.

So all around the air was perfumed with goodness-kindness-charity, all under the influence of the Great Mother's will. And in this heady atmosphere, whenever Nabin Panda thought about Simhavahini, the picture of the full-breasted heavy-hipped Jashoda floated in his mind's eye. He wondered whether the Mother was not appearing before him in the form of Jashoda, just as she appeared in Jashoda's dreams as a midwife. The priest who was entitled to fifty percent of the temple's takings dismissed his fancies with the advice, "You are pixilated. It's a disease that attacks both men and women. You'd better tie the root of a white aparajita on your ear while you are peeing."

Nabin was not prepared to acknowledge this. One day, he told Kangali, "I am a devotee of the Mother, I will not fool around with Shakti. But I have a great idea. There is no harm in Vaishnavite hanky-panky. I tell you. Spread the word that you have found a Gopal in a dream. My aunt brought me a stone image of a Gopal from Shrikshetra Puri. Let me give that to you. The moment it gets around that God has appeared to you as Gopal in a dream, there will be a great big splash and what's more, cash will come clinking in. Begin, because you need the dough, and then you will see that holy thoughts will follow."

Kangali admonished him: "Shame on you, dada, how can

you flim-flam with the gods?" So Nabin shooed him off with a "Go to hell." But subsequent events showed that Kangali would have done well to heed Nabin's advice. For Halderbabu suddenly died of a heart failure. It was the end of the world for Kangali and Jashoda. A Shakespearean welkin broke over their heads.

Halderbabu left Kangali a pauper. All the wishes of the Goddess uttered around Kangali, with Halderbabu as a via media, now disappeared into thin air like the blazing pre-election promises made by political parties, and the couple lost sight of the rosy prospect, just as the flight of a film heroine to some unknown destination in a movie is shrouded by some mysterious magic. The many-colored balloon of Jashoda and Kangali's fantasy burst with a prick from a European witch's bodkin, and the two were utterly stranded.

The children, Gopal, Nepal and Radharani, continuously wailed for food and got a tongue-lashing from their mother. It was quite natural for the little ones to cry with hunger. Ever since Kangalicharan had lost his feet, they were accustomed to nice meals, thanks to the Halder food parcels.

Kangali also yearned for a scoop of rice. But when, in order to divert himself, he induced a feeling of filial love and rubbed his face against Jashoda's breasts like a little Gopal, he got a terrible scolding.

Jashoda was a true example of Indian womanhood. She was typical of a chaste and loving wife and devoted mother, ideals which defy intelligence and rational explanation, which involve sacrifice and dedication stretching the limits of imagination, and which have been kept alive in the popular Indian psyche through the ages, beginning with Sati-Savitri-Sita right down to Nirupa Roy and Chand Usmani in our times. Seeing such a woman, every Tom, Dick and Harry knows that the ancient Indian traditions are alive and kicking. Old sayings celebrating the fortitude of women were made to describe such females.

Actually, Jashoda did not wish to blame her husband one bit for their calamity. The same protective love that welled up within her for her children reached out to envelop her husband. She wanted to be transformed into an Earth Mother, rich in a harvest of fruits and grains, in order to feed her disabled husband and helpless children.

The ancient sages have depicted man and woman as the male and female principles in nature. They never described this maternal emotion that Jashoda felt towards her husband, but then, they, the sages, existed in those long-forgotten times when they first came into this peninsula from other countries. However, such is the chemistry of the soil of this land that all women turn into mothers here and all men choose to be eternal sons. All those who ignore the fact that in this country all men are Balgopals and all women Nandaranis (Krishna's foster mother), and instead look on women in a different light such as 'eternal she,' 'Mona Lisa,' 'L'Apassionata,' 'Simone de Beauvoir' etc., are mere amateurs in the act of pasting current posters over existing, tattered ones.

That is why, one observes, educated Babus harbor such liberated stereotypes about women outside their family fold. The moment these revolutionary women cross the Babu's domestic threshold, the men desire the old Nandarani in words and deeds. It is a complex process. Because Saratchandra understood it very well, he always made his heroines feed the heroes a good meal. The apparent simplicity of Saratchandra and writers of his ilk is, in reality, quite complicated and worthy of calm consideration of an evening while sipping a cold glass of bael panna. (In West Bengal, all those who engage in cerebral and intellectual work strongly experience the grip of amoebic dysentery, and on that account they should give due importance to bael. It is because we do not recognize the importance of traditional herbal medicines in our lives that we do not know what we are losing in the process.)

But let that pass. In recounting Jashoda's life story, we should not make all these detours. The reader's patience is surely not like the potholes of Calcutta's streets, given to increasing by leaps and bounds with every passing decade. The truth of the matter is that Jashoda was caught in a tight spot. After old Halderbabu's last rites were over (during which period the deprived family ate their fill), Jashoda went to meet Halderginni, clutching Radharani at her breast. She wanted to plead her case with the mistress of the house and secure employment with the family as a cook in their vegetarian kitchen.

Halderginni had been heartbroken by her husband's death. But just recently the family lawyer had informed her that the master had left the title deeds of the house and the ownership of the wholesale rice business in her name. And so, heartened by this secret strength, she once again took up the helms of her household. In the beginning she had been very depressed at having to give up the choicest pieces of fish and delicacies such as fish heads. But gradually she found that one can continue to exist with the help of the purest ghee made from cow's milk, rich kheer, the best kinds of bananas, and sweetened curds and sandesh from such well-known shops as Ganguram.

And so, sitting on a stool, Halderginni reigned supreme over her household and glowed with the well-being of her good living and power. Ensconced on her lap was her six-month old grandson. Up to now, six of her sons had been married off, and because the almanac prescribes intercourse with one's wife almost every month, the row of rooms located on the ground floor of her house, which had been specially set aside for confinements, were hardly ever empty. The lady doctor and the midwife, Sarala, were permanent visitors to the household. The old lady had six daughters. They also bred regularly at eighteen-month intervals, and so the Halder home was infested with an epidemic of kanthas and diapers, feeding bottles and pacifiers, rubber sheets and Johnson's Baby powder.

Mrs. Halder was exasperated by the struggle to feed her infant grandson lying on her lap. Seeing Jashoda, she was overcome with relief and exclaimed, "Ma, you are a godsend! Please nurse him a bit, I beg of you. His mother is unwell, and he is such a stubborn creature that he will not touch the bottle."

Jashoda stayed in that house till nine at night. She nursed

the infant at her breast from time to time in answer to the old lady's pleas. The cook was asked to send a generously-filled pot of rice and curry to Jashoda's family.

During the day, while nursing the child, Jashoda posed the question to the mistress of the house: "Ma, the master promised so many things, but he is no longer there and so I don't want to rake up the past. But you know that your poor Brahmin son has been crippled. I don't care about myself. But I worry about my husband and children and it is on their behalf that I am requesting you for a job—any job. Maybe you could employ me in your kitchen."

Halderginni did not feel the same devotion towards Brahmins as her husband, so she replied, "Wait a while. Let me think about it." Halderginni did not quite accept the fact that Kangali's loss of feet was in any way connected with her youngest son's noontime quirks. It was as much a question of Kangali's fate. Otherwise why should he have been walking down that road, smiling euphorically in that blazing noonday sun?

Halderginni cast a sideward glance, filled with both admiration and envy, at Jashoda's mammary projections. She admitted ruefully: "Really! God has created you to be a Kamadhenu, a divine milch-cow. Your tits yield milk with the slightest suck. The creatures whom I have brought into my own house are almost dry. They do not have even a fraction of the milk that you do."

Jashoda acknowledged the compliment with great self-assurance: "That goes without saying, Ma. I remember Gopal was weaned when he was three years old and this little one had not come into my womb then. Even so, my breasts would be flooded with milk. I wonder where it comes from? I am hardly able to take any special care of myself or get any proper nourishment."

At night Jashoda's flowing milkbar was the subject of much heated discussion among the women of the household. And finally, even the men got to hear about it. The second son,

whose wife was unwell and whose infant son was nursed by
Jashoda, was particularly wife-oriented. He differed from his
brothers in that, while they made children with their wives—
after duly consulting the almanac for an auspicious time, and at
that moment filled with love for their spouses, or indifference,
or even disgust, or for that matter preoccupied with the nuts
and bolts of business—the second son made his wife pregnant
with the same frequency, but a deep love for her drove him to it
all the time.

That his wife got big with child repeatedly was all God's
will, but he was eager that she remain good to look at. He had
always worried about how to combine beauty with repeated
childbearing but was at his wit's end regarding a solution. Now
when he heard from his wife about Jashoda's surplus milk
supply, he suddenly exclaimed:

"Ah! I've found a way."

"Way for what?" the wife asked.

"A way to relieve you of your troubles."

"Relieve me of my troubles? How is that possible? My
troubles will be over only when I am on the funeral pyre. How
can my health survive an annual turn of childbed?"

"Your health will recover. It will recover for sure. I have just
discovered a divine machinery. Even though you will have a
child every year your figure will remain perfect."

And so the husband and wife confabulated. In the morning
the husband went to his mother's room and held some serious
discussions with her. She was at first reluctant to heed the son's
whispered suggestion, but when she thought it over for a
while, she felt it was a million rupee proposal. Daughters-in-law
have come into the house and because of the ineluctable laws of
nature, they will become mothers. And as mothers, they will
nurse their babies. Inevitably, they would continue to be mothers as long as it was possible, and it therefore automatically
followed that if they continued to breast-feed, they would lose
their figures. As a result, if her sons did a bit of skirt chasing

outside the house or if they ran after the maidservants at home, she would have no one to blame: it was only natural that they should search for greener pastures outside the house.

So if Jashoda became a wet nurse to all the newborns of the family, the problem would be solved by sending her a daily hamper, giving her clothes for special occasions and paying her a few rupees at the end of every month. Besides, all kinds of rituals were a regular occurrence at her home and a Brahmin woman had a special role to play on such occasions. Jashoda could easily double up. Moreover, Halderginni's son was responsible for Jashoda's plight; this would be a good way of absolving themselves.

When Halderginni made the proposal to Jashoda, the poor woman felt that she had been offered a cabinet ministry. She began to think of her breasts as precious objects. One night when Kangalicharan started making approaches, she warned him, "Look, I will keep the household running on the strength of these. So you had better use them carefully." That night Kangalicharan gave up his usual practice reluctantly. But when he saw the quantity of rice, dal, oil and vegetables in the hamper, he lost all traces of the tender, filial emotions of a Gopal for his mother, and instead became charged as Brahma the Creator.

He explained to Jashoda, "Your breasts will be filled with milk only if there is a child in your womb. Keeping that in mind, you will have to suffer a lot of problems. You are a good woman, a virtuous woman. It is because the Goddess had foreknowledge that you will become pregnant, have children whom you will nurse yourself, that the Great Mother appeared before you as a midwife."

Jashoda appreciated Kangali's arguments and her eyes filled with tears of penitence. She said, "You are my lord and master as well as my teacher, my guru. If I ever forget my place and say no to you, you must correct me. Don't talk of suffering. Where is the suffering in childbearing? Didn't Halderginnima have thirteen deliveries? Does a tree suffer when bearing fruit?"

And so that rule was established. Kangalicharan became a professional father while Jashoda became a professional mother. In fact, looking at Jashoda, the greatest skeptic was converted into ardently believing the message of that famous Bengali devotion song which goes something like this: "It isn't easy to be a mother/Just having kids isn't enough."

On the ground floor of the Halder house, around the huge square courtyard, some dozen or so healthy cows of fine breed were always kept tied to their stakes. Two Bhojpuris, considering them to be Sacred Mothers, tended them very carefully. Mounds of grass, fodder, cattlefeed, oilcakes and molasses were brought to the house for them. Halderginni was of the opinion that the milk yield of the cows would increase in proportion to their feed.

But now, Jashoda's position in the household was even more exalted than those sacred creatures, the more so because Halderginni's sons created offspring like Brahma, the creator of the world. And Jashoda nurtured them. The old lady kept a strict check on things so that nothing stemmed her milk supply. One day she called Kangalicharan and told him, "Look son, in the sweet shop you were accustomed to preparing food. Why don't you take charge of the cooking at home now and give my girl a little rest? She has two of her own and there are three kids here. After nursing five, is it possible for her to go home and cook?"

Wisdom dawned on Kangalicharan, and when he came down, the two Bhojpuris gave him a pinch of tobacco to chew and exclaimed, "The mistress is quite right! Just watch how we look after our sacred cows whom we treat as our mothers, and your wife, she is mother to the whole world!"

Kangalicharan started cooking for the family, and made his children his assistants. In time, he perfected the most difficult delicacies of Bengali cuisine, such as the special dals, the sweet and sour fish, and the dried vegetable preparation from the plantain tree trunk. He even prepared a fabulous curry from the sacrificial goat head from the temple of Simhavahini, and made his way into the heart of the drunk and dope-addicted Nabin through his stomach. As a result Nabin fixed him up in the Nakuleshwar Shiva temple.

Jashoda started bloating up like a Public Works Department officer's bank account as a result of being served hot, ready-cooked meals at home. Besides, Halderginni allotted her a daily drink of milk, and whenever she started expecting a child, the old lady sent her pickles, chutneys, relishes and preserves. Even the unbelievers started toying with the idea that only for this had the goddess Simhavahini appeared in Jashoda's dreams as a midwife with a bag under her arm. Otherwise who on earth had ever heard of or seen such repeated pregnancies and deliveries, this unlimited nursing of other people's children, yielding milk like a great cow. All the dirty fantasizing that Nabin had been indulging in about Jashoda vanished. Imbibing such stimulating stuff as ritual spirit, hash and spicy curried goat's head did not help to excite Nabin's cooling ardor. Instead, he was filled with an emotion close to piety, so that whenever he met Jashoda, he addressed her as mother. Consequently, there was a revival of faith in the whole area in the greatness of Simhavahini, and the electrifying currents of that faith filled the air in the locality.

Everyone's respect and devotion towards Jashoda became so intense that she started playing a prominent part in all the womanly rituals connected with marriage, childbirth, thread ceremony, and so on. The special feelings towards Jashoda were now extended to her offspring: her sons, Nepal, Gopal, Neno, Boncha and Patel, began to don the sacred thread as they grew up and started touting for pilgrims visiting the temple. Kangali did not have to search for grooms for his daughters, Radharani, Altarani and Padmarani. Nabin found husbands for them with great alacrity and the chaste daughters of a chaste mother, like the true satis that they were, went to make homes for their Shivas.

Jashoda's worth increased in the Halder household. Nowadays, the daughters-in-law did not get weak with alarm when they saw their husbands consult the almanac, and this in itself pleased the sons of the house. They could act the eternal child, Gopal, in bed because their own children were being nursed at Jashoda's breasts; the wives had no grounds to reject their advances.

The wives in turn were happy because they could keep their figures in shape. They could wear cholis of fashionable cut and bras in the latest styles. On Shivaratri, they could watch films the whole night because they didn't have to bother about feeding their babes, and all this was possible because of Jashoda.

Inevitably Jashoda was filled with a sense of her own importance and began taking the liberty of voicing her opinions. She would be sitting in the old lady's room, feeding the infants endlessly while making sarcastic comments like, "Women are made to have babies. Whoever has heard of calling in doctors, checking blood pressures, having tonics prescribed for something so natural! Great big fusspots if you ask me. Look at me. Here I am, a baby every year. Is it affecting my health or drying up the milk? Disgraceful! Here they are having the milk dried up with injections! Never heard of such a shameful thing in my life."

It had been the custom in the Halder household that the boys, as soon as they were in their teens, started making passes at the maidservants in the house. This pattern changed with the present generation of adolescents. They had been nursed by Jashoda and thought of her as a mother-substitute. Now they adopted the same attitude towards the other women servants in the household and, instead, started hanging around the girls' school. Relieved of their unwanted attention, the maids acclaimed Jashoda saying, "Joshi, you are great. It is because of you that the whole household has changed."

One day, the youngest Halder son was squatting in front of Jashoda and watching her nurse an infant, when she addressed him: "Son you have brought me an enormous amount of luck. It was because you crippled my man that all these comforts came to me. Can you tell me whose will all this is?"

The boy replied, "It is Mother Simhavahini's." He wanted to know very badly how the legless Kangali played the role of Brahma, but since the conversation turned to matters spiritual, he forgot to raise the question. It was all the will of Simhavahini.

Kangali's legs were amputated in the fifties. From then we have reached present times. In the intervening twenty-five years or, to be more precise, say, thirty years, Jashoda had taken to childbed some twenty times. The last few pregnancies did not serve their purpose because, somehow, fresh winds of change started blowing away the old cobwebs in the Halder household. But let me first deal with the major events of the intervening years.

When this story started Jashoda was the mother of three. After that she had seventeen confinements. Meanwhile, old Halderginni also died. The old lady played one favorite wishing game: she wanted at least one of her daughters-in-law to have the same sort of experience that she had had. It was customary in the family that if one had twenty children the couple had to go through the entire wedding ceremony once again, with all the related pomp and circumstance.

But Halderginni's daughters-in-law were not prepared to fulfill this desire. They cried halt after a dozen or so. Thanks to some unfortunate wicked thinking on their part, they were able to convince their husbands and went into hospitals to take the necessary steps. All this was the fault of new trends sweeping through society.

Through the ages, thinkers and sages have never allowed the winds of change to enter the citadel of the family. My grandmother used to tell me the story of a respectable gentleman who came to her house to read through the rather startling literary magazine, *Sanibarer Chithi*. He would not dream of allowing the journal into his own home! "The moment wives, mothers, and sisters start reading that magazine, they will claim

that they are women first and last, not mothers, sisters, wives."
And if he was asked what would happen as a result, he would
reply, "They will start cooking meals wearing slippers in the
kitchen." It is an age-old custom: new fashions, new fads always destroy domestic peace.

The sixteenth century continued to reign in the Halder
household, but suddenly, because of a proliferation of family
members, some of the men broke away from the joint family
and set up households of their own in other localities. They flew
the nest. Even this could be tolerated, but what was most
objectionable was that the old lady's granddaughters-in-law
came into the family with completely different notions of Motherhood from Halderginni's.

In vain the old lady argued that there was no lack of food or
cash. The old master had had a secret dream of filling up half of
Calcutta with Halders. But the younger women were unwilling
to oblige. Defying the old lady, they discarded the family home-
stead and accompanied their husbands to their places of work.
Meanwhile, following a fracas among the temple priests, an
unidentified person or group turned the Simhavahini image
around.

The news of the goddess turning her face away broke the
old lady's heart, and one midsummer day, after eating an enormous quantity of overripe jackfruit, she died of gastroenteritis.
In dying, the old lady found her release. The burden of living
was far more irksome than passing over to the other side.
Jashoda grieved over Halderginni's death, really and truly.
Basini, the long-time maidservant of the household, was well
known in the locality for her professional mourning, but with
Mrs. Halder's expiry, Jashoda surprised everyone with the ve-
hemence of her performance. The reason of course, was that
with the departure of Halderginni, Jashoda would lose her meal
ticket.

Basini howled, "Oh Ma! Where are you now? Ma, you had
such a fill of good fortune! You were the jewel in the crown after
the master's death! It was you who kept a tight control and held

everything together! Ma! What sins have we committed that you should leave us? I pleaded with you not to eat so much jackfruit, but you paid no heed!"

Jashoda bided her time and when Basini paused to catch her breath, she wailed with redoubled strength, "Ma! Why should you remain here? You, who were so blessed, why should you put up with this sinful world? There was a throne established here for you to reign but then your daughters-in-law discarded it. Isn't it a terrible sin for the tree to refuse to bear fruit? Is it possible that a virtuous woman like you can tolerate such evil? And to top it all Simhavahini turned her face away, Ma. You realized that a virtuous home has turned into an ungodly den. Is it conceivable that you could go on living here? After the master had left this world, I could see that you also wanted to join him. But I realized that in the interests of your family, you kept your body and soul together."

Jashoda addressed the daughters-in-law, weeping as she did so, "Get some alta and take her footprints. Those footprints will act as a talisman for your family. The goddess Lakshmi will never desert the household as long as the footprints are there. Every morning if you do your obeisance there before starting the day, it will ward off all sickness and disaster."

Jashoda followed the funeral procession to the burning ghat, weeping and wailing at the loss of her employer. When she returned, she claimed emphatically, "Saw it with my own eyes, cross my heart. A chariot came down from heaven and snatched the mistress's body right out of the funeral pyre and whisked it upwards in a matter of seconds."

After the last rites and prescribed period of mourning were over, the eldest daughter-in-law spoke to Jashoda, "Bamin didi, I must talk to you. The family is breaking up. The second and third brother's families are moving into the Beliaghata house. The fourth and the fifth are shifting to Maniktala-Bagmari. The youngest will be setting up his home in our house in Dakshineswar."

"Who will stay here?"

"We are going to stay put here. But we will be renting out the ground floor rooms. We will reduce our establishment and cut expenditure. We must. You have been wet nurse to the family, you have nursed the children, and in return, a daily hamper of food had been sent to your house. Even after the last child had been weaned, my mother-in-law continued to send you the food parcel for eight years. She did as she pleased and her sons never objected. But I will not be able to continue in the same style!"

"What will happen to me, Boudi?"

"If you cook and look after the kitchen for my family, you will make enough to support yourself. But what about the rest at home? What will you do about them?"

"What shall I do?"

"It is for you to say. You are the mother of twelve living children. The girls have been married off. The boys, I am told, help to bring pilgrims to the temple. They also eat the temple prasad and sleep in the courtyard. The Brahmin, your man, I hear is doing quite well at the Nakuleswar temple. What is your problem? You do not have to worry about anything."

Jashoda wiped her eyes and murmured, "Let me see. I will speak to my husband."

Kangalicharan's temple was a scene of hectic activity. He brusquely asked Jashoda, "What will you do in my temple?"

"What does Nabin's niece do?"

"She looks after the temple household, cooks the prasad. You have not done any cooking for so long even at home. How can you look after the heavy kitchen work of the temple?"

"The food parcels are going to be stopped. Has that entered your thick head, you bum? What will you do for a meal?"

Kangali answered, "You don't have to worry about that."

"Why did you let me do the worrying for so long? A lot of money seems to be rolling in at the temple, isn't that so? You have saved every bit of it and lived like a parasite on my hard work."

"Who did the cooking at home?"

Jashoda answered with a contemptuous gesture, "The men bring in the food, the women cook. That is the age-old pattern. But in my case everything is reversed. You have lived off me all these years, so now you feed me. That is only right."

Kangali retorted sharply, "How did you manage to get the food in the first place? Would you have had entry into the Halder home? You were lucky to have the doors opened to you only because I lost my legs. You seem to have forgotten everything, you hussy."

"Hussy yourself! Living off his wife and calls himself a man."

Following this, the two got into a terrible fight. Invectives and curses flowed fast and furious between them, and at last Kangali exploded: "Beat it! I don't want to see your face again."

"So you don't want to see me again, do you? That's fine by me." Jashoda left the room in a rage. Meanwhile, the various shareholding priests in the temple had discussed the urgent need to restore the goddess to her old position, and so a puja of atonement was being celebrated with great pomp in the temple.

Jashoda threw herself at the feet of the goddess. Her grief seemed to burst through her flabby, middle-aged, milk-dried breasts. She wanted Mother Simhavahini to understand her hopeless state and to show her the way out of her misery.

For three days and nights Jashoda lay prone in the temple courtyard. But Simhavahini herself must have been affected by all the new ways, the changes in the air, for she did not bother to appear in Jashoda's dreams. In fact, when Jashoda went home, shivering with weakness after three days of fasting, her youngest son informed her, "Father says he will stay in the temple. He has asked me and Naba to ring the bells there. He says we will get some money and can eat the prasad."

"I see. Where is your father?"

"He is lying down. Golapi Masi is scratching the prickly heat rash on his back. He gave us some money to buy lollipops and leave him alone. So I ran home to tell you."

Jashoda realized that it was not just the Halder household

but Kangali also who had outgrown the need for her. After quieting her gnawing hunger with a drink of water and a bit of candy sugar, she went out to complain to Nabin. It was he who had turned the Simhavahini image around, and after negotiating satisfactorily with the other priests on the division of the takings on special festival days, he reinstated the image to her original position. As a result, he had massaged his aching body with alcohol and was high on hash. He was busy hectoring the local candidate for the elections with dire threats: "You did not bother to make your special offerings. The Mother's powers have returned. Let's see how you win this time."

That the days of miracles were not yet over and extended to the temple precincts can be evidenced from Nabin himself. It was he who had turned the image because he felt that the priests were not aligning themselves into a united front like the political parties before elections, and afterwards had begun to believe that the goddess had turned her face away. And now that the image had been reestablished, he made himself believe that she had returned of her own accord. Jashoda accosted him, "What rubbish are you talking?"

"I am talking of the greatness and powers of the Devi," replied Nabin.

Jashoda was still aggressive. "You think I don't know that it was you who turned the goddess around?"

Nabin shushed her: "Shut up, Joshi. Wasn't it the goddess who gave me the strength and the imagination? Otherwise how could I have carried it out?"

"It was in your hands that the goddess lost her powers," Joshoda stated flatly.

"Lost her powers! Pah! There is a fan circulating over your head, and you are enjoying that cool breeze. Has it happened before? Have you ever had an electric fan in the temple court-yard?"

"Hmm. A likely story. But tell me, what have I done to you? Why have you ruined my life, destroyed my future?"

"What's the matter? Kangali is not dead."

"Why should he kick the bucket? Oh no! It's much worse than that."

"What has happened?"

Jashoda wiped her eyes and spoke in a voice choking with unshed tears, "I have given birth to so many and that is why I was the permanent wet nurse in the Halder household, the overflowing milk bar. It is not that you do not know everything. I have never strayed, always on the straight and narrow."

"God bless me. How can you utter such things. You are the great Mother's incarnation."

"Well, the Mother has done pretty well by herself, what with offerings and worship. But the incarnation is about to die of starvation. The Halder meals are drying up."

"But why did you have to go and pick a quarrel with Kangali? After all he is a man. How do you expect him to react when you flaunt the fact that you have been the breadwinner?"

"True, but why did you have to plant your niece there?"

"That, after all, is the will of the goddess. Golapi used to go to the temple for darshan and pray for hours. Gradually Kangali realized that he was Bhairav and she his Bhairavi in the true tantrik tradition."

"Bhairavi be hanged! Even now I can horsewhip her and drag my husband away."

Nabin exclaimed, "That is not possible any longer. Kangali is a virile man. You won't be able to satisfy him any longer. Besides Golapi's brother is a notorious goonda. He is keeping guard there. He even threw me out. If I smoke ten drags of hash, he smokes twenty. Gave me one kick in my ass. I had gone to plead your case. Kangali would not listen. Said not to mention your name. 'She does not appreciate her husband but runs after her employer's family. The employers are her gods. Let her go there.' "

"Fine, that is what I will do."

With this parting shot, Jashoda, half-crazed by the injustices meted out to her by life, returned home. But it was difficult for her to settle down in the empty house. She felt desolate; it was difficult to fall asleep without a child curled up against her. Motherhood is a terrible addiction; once you are hooked it is difficult to withdraw even after the milk has run dry.

Swallowing her self-respect, Jashoda appealed to Mrs. Halder, the new mistress of the household. She said, "I'll cook and serve. If you wish to pay me, well and good, if not, then don't. But you will have to let me stay here. That good-for-nothing husband of mine is living in the temple. And the kids, they are such ungrateful wretches, Ma, they have joined him. For whom then should I keep maintaining the room?"

"You may stay here," said the new mistress generously. "You have nursed the young ones and, on top of that, you are a Brahmin. Stay. But I must warn you, it will be difficult for you. You will have to share the same room with Basini and the rest. You will have to learn to adjust and not quarrel with anyone. As you know, Babu, the new master is hot-tempered. To make matters worse the third son has gone to Bombay and married a local chit. So already he is nettled. If there are squabbles to add to all this, he will be beside himself."

Jashoda's fertility had been her fortune. With that over, she had her first brush with hard times. The chaste, respected Jashoda, rich in her milk yield, cherished by all the local mothers, now found her luck was down. But human nature is contrary. During bad times, one is not prepared to swallow one's overweening pride and accept with humility the raw deal meted out by life. And so, buoyed by an old arrogance, one is ready to pick a fight over small issues only to have one's nose rubbed in the dirt by the lowliest.

Jashoda suffered the same fate. In the old days, Basini and the rest had been real boot lickers, ready to fawn on her for her favors. Now Basini declared without batting an eyelid, "You wash your own plate and glass. Are you my employer that I should do your menial work for you? You are a servant the same as me. No difference."

"Don't forget who I am," shouted Jashoda in a rage. But

she was put in her place by the new mistress. "This is what I was afraid of," she said, "my mother-in-law has pampered her no end. Listen didi, I did not beg you to join my service, you came on your own. So now keep to yourself and don't make trouble."

Jashoda realized that she no longer had a voice in the household. No one was prepared to listen to anything she had to say. Keeping her counsel she cooked and served and when evening came she went to the temple yard and silently shed tears of bitterness. She could not even lighten her burden by crying openly. After the evening worship at the Nakuleshwar temple was over and Jashoda had heard the drums and bells and cymbals, she wiped her eyes and returned home. She whispered, "Have mercy on me, Great Mother. In the end do I have to sit on the roadside with a tin bowl begging for alms? Is that what you want?"

Jashoda could have spent the rest of her days cooking for the Halders and unburdening her sorrows at the temple. But fate had decreed otherwise. She began to feel that her body could not cope any longer. She could not quite put her finger on why she felt so depressed. Her mind became confused. While she was cooking she was constantly assailed by the thought that she had been the wet nurse in this household.

Images float through her mind. She remembers going home with the food hamper wearing a wide-bordered sari. Her breasts feel empty, wasted. She had never dreamt that there would come a time when no babies would suck at her nipples.

She became absentminded. She cooked and served the meals but forgot to eat herself. Sometimes she would appeal to Nakuleshwar Shiva. "If Mother does not take me back herself, you must put an end to all my troubles. Take me back. I can't bear to live any longer."

In the end it was the new mistress's sons who informed their mother, "Ma, is our nurse ill? She does not seem to be herself."

"I'll take a look," she assured them.

Her husband interjected, "Yes, you should. After all she is a Brahmin and if something happens to her the sin would be laid at our door."

The mistress went to find out. She saw that Jashoda had put the rice on the stove to cook, spread out a part of her sari on the kitchen floor and was lying down.

Seeing her exposed body, the lady of the house exclaimed, "Oh dear, didi. What is that red patch on your breast, Good God! It's such an angry red."

"God only knows what it is. It's big and hard like a pebble and feels as hard as stone."

"What is wrong?"

"I wouldn't know. Maybe this is the result of all those infants that I suckled."

"Rubbish! You get such inflammations only when there is milk in your breast. But even your youngest is at least ten years old."

"Oh, the youngest is no longer there. He passed away soon after birth, and a good thing too. It's a wicked world."

"Wait, tomorrow the doctor is coming to examine my grandson. I'll ask him. It doesn't look right to me."

Jashoda closed her eyes in pain and said, "It feels like a breast made of stone or filled with stones. Earlier the hard lump used to move about, now the whole breast feels heavy and inert."

"Shall I ask the doctor to take a look?"

"Oh no! No Boudi, I won't be able to expose myself before a male doctor."

That night the doctor came. Using her son as a via media, the lady recounted Jashoda's problems. "There is no pain or burning, but for some reason she seems to be getting more and more listless."

The doctor inquired, "Find out if the nipple is crinkled and if there are glands under the arm like a swollen ball."

Hearing such words as nipple and ball, the lady thought to

herself, "How crude," but she went to investigate on the spot. She returned to report, "The woman says that she has had these symptoms that you mention for a long time."

"How old is she?"

"If you count from the age of the eldest son, she should be fifty-five."

"I'll prescribe some medicine," the doctor said. On his way out he told the master of the house, "I hear there is something wrong with your cook's breast. I think it would a good idea to take her to the cancer hospital for a checkup. I have not seen her personally, but from all that I hear it could a cancer of the mammary gland."

Until very recently, the eldest Halder had been living in the sixteenth century. He had entered the twentieth century only a very little while ago. Of his thirteen children, he had married off his daughters; his sons had grown up, or were growing up, and making their own way in life according to their lights. But even now Mr. Halder's brain cells were steeped in the dark ignorance of pre-Bengal renaissance days.

He still would not get vaccinated against smallpox, saying, "Smallpox attacks the lower classes. I don't need to be vaccinated. In upper-class families, among those who respect the gods and Brahmins, such filthy diseases never occur."

He pooh-poohed the suggestion of cancer contemptuously: "Huh! Of all things, cancer! Highly unlikely. God alone knows what was said and what you heard. Go and prescribe some ointment and I am sure it will heal. I am not prepared to send a Brahmin woman to the hospital on your say-so."

On hearing the word hospital, Jashoda also refused, saying, "Surely I will not be able to go there. It would be far easier for me to give up my life. I did not go to the hospital for all these childbirths, and now you want me to go there? It was only because that rotter went to the hospital that he returned minus his two legs."

Mrs. Halder replied, "Let me bring you some magic ointment prepared by a sadhu. It is sure to bring relief. The suppressed boil will come to a head and burst."

But the panacea and magic balm failed to work. In time Jashoda lost her appetite and could not eat. She grew progressively weaker. She could not cover her left breast any longer with the end of her sari. Sometimes she thought it was burning, at other times she felt sore. There were lesions on the skin and the whole area became an open sore. Jashoda took to her bed.

Seeing these developments Mr. Halder became nervous. He was afraid that a Brahmin woman would die under his roof and the sin be visited on him. He called Jashoda's sons and scolded them, "It is your own mother and she has brought you up and looked after you for so long and now she is dying. You had better take her with you. Is it right that when she has all of you, she should die in a Kayastha house?"

Kangali cried copiously when he heard this. He came to visit Jashoda, lying in her room in semidarkness. He pleaded with her, "Wife, you were chaste as Sita and good as Lakshmi. I have suffered for ill-treating you. Within two years after the temple plates were stolen, I had boils on my back and that bitch Golapi got around Nepal and broke open the cash box. She made off with the money and set up shop in Tarakeshwar. Come home and I will look after you. I'll do all I can to keep you in comfort."

Jashoda listened and then said quietly, "Light the lamp." Kangali lit the oil lamp.

Jashoda showed him her bare, ulcerated left breast. "Have you seen the sore?" she asked, "Do you know the stench it gives out? What will you do with me if you take me home now? And in any case why did you come now to take me back?"

"The master told us to."

"Ah! Then the master does not want to keep me here any longer." Jashoda sighed and said, "I will not be of any earthly use to anyone, how will you manage if you take me back?"

"It doesn't matter. I'll take you home tomorrow. Today I will clean out the room. Tomorrow I'll take you back, as sure as I am standing here."

"Are the boys all right? Before, Nawal and Gour used to drop in occasionally. But now even they have stopped coming."

"Selfish bastards, each one of them. After all, they are born of my seed. No wonder they are heartless like me."

"Will you come tomorrow?"

"I will, I will, I will, I promise."

Suddenly Jashoda smiled. It was a wistful smile of the kind which touches the core of one's being and revives memories. She asked shyly, "Do you remember?"

"Remember what, my dear?"

"Remember how you used to caress these breasts? You could not close your eyes otherwise. My lap was never empty and there would be a never-ending line of infants to suckle. On top of that there would be the babies of the master's family whom I had to nurse. How did I manage, I wonder."

"I remember everything, my dear."

At that moment Kangali meant what he said. Seeing Jashoda's diseased, worn-out body, pity welled up in the greedy, self-centered, self-indulgent Kangali to whom his own physical gratification had always been of prime importance. Stirred by a deep sadness, he held Jashoda's hand and remarked, "You have a fever?"

"Yes, I always have a fever. I think it is because of the inflammation."

"Where is this awful stink coming from?"

"From my wound," Jashoda answered, closing her eyes. Then she added, "Perhaps you had better call in Sannyasi doctor. He cured Gopal's typhoid with homeopathic medicine."

"I'll call him. I'll take you home tomorrow itself."

Kangali left that day. But Jashoda could not hear the tap-tapping of his crutch when he went out. With her eyes closed, thinking Kangali was still in the room, she whispered softly, "It is all lies what they say, that you are a mother if you suckle a baby. Look at me. The boys, Nepal, Gopal and the rest hardly bother to come in and neither do the boys in the Halder family make any inquiries about my health. No one cares."

The multiple lesions on Jashoda's cancerous breast, open and oozing, seemed to ridicule her sorrow. "Listen," she called, and opened her eyes, but realized that Kangali had gone away.

That night she got Basini to buy her a cake of Lifebuoy soap and had a bath the next morning. What a foul smell, a god-awful stink. It's the kind of fetid smell that one gets when carcasses of cats and dogs rot in the neighborhood garbage cans. All her life, because she had had to nurse the children of the Halders, Jashoda had looked after her breasts, massaging them with oil and cleaning the nipples with soap and water. Those breasts that she had cared for so well had in the end betrayed her. She wonderd why.

Her skin burned when it came in contact with the harsh soap. Even so, Jashoda soaped herself thoroughly. But when she finished her head was swimming, her eyes were blurred, and everything became dim around her. Her head and body seemed to be on fire. The black floor looked so inviting and cool. Jashoda spread one end of her sari on the floor and lay down. Her breasts seemed to weigh a ton and she could not continue standing under their weight.

The moment she lay down, she lost all consciousness. Kangali came the next day just as he had promised. But seeing Jashoda's condition he lost his head and did not know what to do. At last Nabin came and shouted, "Are these people fit to call themselves human beings? Here was this woman who nursed all their babies and they could not even call a doctor. I'll go and call Hari doctor just now."

The moment Hari doctor saw the patient he declared, "Hospital!"

Normally patients in such extreme conditions are not admitted, but Jashoda got in through Halderbabu's efforts and influence.

"What has happened? Oh daktarbabu, please tell me what has happened?" cried Kangali like a little boy.

"Cancer!"

"Is it possible to have cancer in the breast?"

"How else did it happen?"

"Twenty of her own and at least thirty from the Halder household. She had a lot of milk daktarbabu."

"What did you say? How many has she nursed?"

"Oh! Fifty easily."

"Fifty?"

"Yes sir."

"She has had twenty children?"

"Yes sir."

"God!"

"Sir?"

"What do you want?"

"Did this happen because she suckled so many?"

"That cannot be said for certain. No one can say what is the cause of cancer. However, those who do a lot of breastfeed-ing. . . . Why did you not realize her state earlier? This could not have happened in one day."

"She was not living with me, sir. There was a quarrel. . . ."

"OK. I have understood."

"How do you see her? Will she get well?"

"Get well? Start counting the days before she goes. You have brought her here at the last stage. No one comes out of this alive."

Kangali returned home crying. In the evening, distressed by his tears and laments, Halderbabu's second son went and talked to the doctor. The boy was not in the least anxious about Jashoda but he went because his father gave him a dressing down and he was still economically dependent on him.

The doctor explained everything. Something like this did not come up suddenly, it developed over a long period of time. How did it happen? No one can say for sure. How can one find out if there is breast cancer? First there is a small lump which can move about. Then the lump gets harder, bigger and spreads over a large area inside the breast. The skin on the surface is likely to get reddish just as the crinkling of the nipple is a possible symptom. The gland in the armpit may get inflamed. Ulceration occurs in the last stage. Fever? That takes second or third place in the order of importance of symptoms. If there is an open sore on the body, temperature is only natural; it's a secondary symptom.

The boy was quite confused by all this expert explaining and could only ask, "Will she live?"

"No."

"Then how long will she suffer?"

"Oh! I don't think it will be very long now."

"But if there is no hope, how will you treat her?"

"I'll prescribe some painkillers, sedatives, and some antibiotics for the fever. Physically, she is very run down."

"She had stopped eating."

"Didn't you call in a doctor?"

"Yes, we did."

"Did he not say anything?"

"He did."

"What was his diagnosis?"

"He said that possibly it was cancer. He suggested that we take her to a hospital. She refused."

"Why should she want to go to a hospital? In that case how can she die?"

The second son came home and reported, "That time when Arun daktar said she had cancer, if we had taken her to the hospital then, she may have lived."

Angry at the implicit accusation, the mother shouted, "If you knew so much then why didn't you take her there? Did I forbid you to?"

Somehow in the minds of the mother and son, an indefinable sense of guilt and remorse came to a head and broke instantly like the gaseous eruptions bubbling on the surface of dank, scummy, stagnant waters. The sense of guilt kept drilling the words into the mind, "She was living under our roof. We did not even bother to look in and see how she was. God alone knows when the illness started, never gave it any importance. She did not know what was happening. After all, she looked after so many of us and we did not look after her in return. And now, when she has so many people to call her own, she has gone to die in a hospital. So many sons, a husband, but she clung to us, and so it was our responsibility! What a strong body she had, what enviable health! The milk would simply spill out of her breasts. Never for a moment did one think that she would be struck with a disease like this."

But the next moment, a more reassuring justification took over: "Who can overrule fate? She was destined to die of cancer; no one can set aside one's fate. If she were to die here, the blame would fall on us. Her husband and children would ask questions about her death. Now we have been saved from that blame. No one can say anything."

Halderbabu senior also reassured them, saying, "Arun daktar has told me that no one can survive an attack of cancer. Since didi had cancer, the doctors would do surgery and remove her breasts and uterus but even after all this people die of cancer. See here, father used to give them due respect because they were Brahmins and we are managing to exist because of father's blessings. If didi died here, we would have to do special pujas of atonement because a Brahmin would have died within our own household."

Patients admitted into the hospital in a far less advanced stage of cancer have died much sooner. Jashoda, to the great surprise of her doctors, lived on for a month longer. In the beginning, Kangali, her sons, and Nabin used to visit her regularly, but Jashoda's condition continued unchanged—comatose, burning with fever, senseless. The sores were getting bigger and bigger and the whole breast took on the appearance of one big naked wound. Although dressed with surgical gauze soaked in antiseptic, the decaying odor from the rotting flesh spiraled through the room and filled it like the perfumed smoke from a burning agarbatti.

Kangali's first flush of concern ebbed somewhat after seeing all this. He said to the doctor, "She doesn't respond to our call."

"Isn't that better? One can hardly bear this excrutiating pain when one is unconscious. It would be impossible to live with it when conscious."

"Does she know that we are coming to visit her?"

"That's difficult to say."

"Is she eating anything?"

"Through tubes and drips."

"Can people live like that?"

"Why this interest now?"

The doctor realized that his irrational anger was caused by Jashoda's condition. His rage covered Jashoda, Kangali, all those women who did not take the early symptoms of breast cancer seriously and suffered such terrible agonies in the end.

Kangali left the room since he did not get a satisfactory answer to his questions. He came to the temple and told Nabin and his sons, "There is no point in going to the hospital and visiting her. She does not recognize anyone, does not open her eyes, does not even know who is coming and going. The doctor is doing everything he can."

"If she dies . . ." ventured Nabin.

"Halderbabu's telephone number is with them. They will inform us."

"Just suppose she wants to see you one last time, Kangali. She has been a good wife to you, completely devoted. Who would say that she was the mother of so many? Her body—but she never strayed, never glanced at another man, not for a moment."

After this outburst, Nabin shut up and sank into himself, ruminating. In fact, since seeing Jashoda lying unconscious with the sores on her breasts exposed, many philosophical thoughts crossed Nabin's mind, aided by a whole host of stimulants, like the rhythmic swaying of mating snakes. Thoughts like—there was such yearning, such longing for her—god, what an end to those beautiful, fascinating breasts—Dammit! The human body is nothing—anyone who loses his balance over it is mad to begin with.

Kangali had no time for Nabin's advice. There was already a sense of rejection in his mind as far as Jashoda was concerned. He was genuinely concerned for her when he first saw her that evening in the Halder house and during the first few days in the hospital, but gradually there was a cooling off of the first welling of compassion. The moment the doctor said that Jashoda would not live, Kangali dismissed her from his mind without a twinge of pain. Her sons were his sons also. Moreover, a distance had already grown between the mother and the sons. The mother they had known, a woman of strong personality, her hair tied high into a neat topknot, her dazzling white sari, was not the same woman lying prostrate on the hospital bed.

The comatose brain as a result of the breast cancer was a welcome relief for Jashoda. She realized that she was in the hospital, and she also realized that this torpor, this state of oblivion, was induced by drugs. She was greatly relieved. And in her weakened condition, her dazed mind wondered whether one of the Halder boys had become a doctor. He must have been suckled by her and was repaying the debt by making her last days comfortable. But the boys of that family go into business as soon as they finish school. Whatever it is, why don't they release her from this foul smell rising up from her breast? What an unbelievable stink, what a betrayal. Knowing that these breasts were her tools of trade, how diligently she strove to keep them filled with milk. After all, that was what a breast was for—to contain milk. How she washed and kept them clean with good toilet soap. She never wore a blouse even when she was young because her breasts were so heavy.

When the effect of the sedation wore off, Jashoda screamed with pain, "A-a-a-a-i-ee," and, with clouded eyes, she looked desperately for the doctor and the nurse. When the doctor came, she muttered in a hurt tone, "You have grown so big on my milk and now you are making me suffer like this."

"She sees the whole world as her nursling," the doctor observed. Then once more an injection, and once again the cherished oblivion. Pain, tormenting pain, the spreading cancer at the expense of the human host. In the course of time the open sore on Jashoda's breast took on the appearance of a volcanic crater. The emanating stench made it difficult to go near her.

Finally, one night Jashoda felt that her hands and feet were getting cold. She realized that death was approaching. She could not open her eyes but she understood that someone was feeling her hands. The prick of an injection needle on her arm. Difficulty in breathing. Inevitable. Who were the people looking after her? Were they her own people?

Jashoda thought that she had nursed her own children because she had brought them into the world; she had nursed the Halder children for a living; she had nursed the whole world. In that case would they let her die alone, unaccompanied? The doctor who was treating her, the one who would pull the sheet over her face, the attendant who would take her out on a trolley, the man who would place her on the funeral pyre, and the dom who would burn her earthly remains, were all her foster children. One had to be a Jashoda to nurse the world. One also had to die alone, friendless, without a single person whom one could call one's own to hold one's hand at the end and to make the last journey easier. But wasn't there a promise or something of someone being there with her at the last moment? Who could it have been? Who? Who?

Jashoda died that night at eleven o'clock.

A phone call was made to Halderbabu's house, but they disconnected their phone at night: it did not ring.

After lying in the morgue as per the rules, Jashoda Devi, Hindu female, was carted in due course to the cremation grounds and cremated in good time. The dom burned her. Whatever Jashoda had thought had come true. She was like God in this respect: whatever was in her mind was executed by others. This time also was no exception; Jashoda's death was god's death. In this world, it has always happened that when a

person takes on godhood upon himself, he is rejected by everyone and is left to die alone.

Translated from the original Bengali
by Ella Dutta

Ila Mehta ▰▰▰ *(Gujarati)*

Smoke

*B*a comes back this evening by the five o'clock train.
Shubha glanced at her watch. It was only four o'clock, still some
time to go. A vast sea of overpowering emptiness engulfed her
being. Nothing left to do. Nothing . . . except wait.

Her hands wandered over the books lying on the table and
picked one up. It was a fat book written in English, on women's
health problems and their treatments. It opened with the picture of a naked woman, bared in vivid detail, sketched with
dexterity. For clinical purposes only, of course!

She slammed it shut, pushed it back and walked out of the
room onto the open balcony. She stood still. The oppressive,
tormenting afternoon was still astride the earth, its heat per-
meating every nook and cranny. "Like my own emptiness," she
thought. "Not a hollow neutral vacuum but this leaden emptiness, opaque and solid.

"The russet evening shall wax but a few moments only.
And then all will be dark again." A wan smile on her lips,
Shubha stepped back into the room.

Just half past four. Driving her car towards the station, Dr.
Shubha scolded herself, "You're becoming neurotic, Shubha.
The sun itself looks like a dark blot to you."

Suddenly her belly tightened. Was everything shipshape
for Ba's homecoming? All details seen to? Like unwinding a reel
of film, she went over the house slowly, room by room, in her

mind's eye. Nothing amiss. All in order. Each corner had been cleaned with care. But suppose? . . . Well—her practice and the clinic really left her with no time to spare. Her mother-in-law knew it well. And those few snatched private moments, well, forget it. It's just as well Ba did not know.

Swiftly, suddenly, a cold shiver rose from the pit of her stomach to her throat, with a chilling reminder—the picture! The photograph of Subodh had been left undusted, with the dirty gray string of dried flowers hanging around it. She had forgotten to place a fresh wreath. And with it remained Bapuji's photograph, too. Ba would of course go straight up to them, first thing on coming home.

Framed in dry dead petals, Subodh's face smiled unmoving in black and white—like the printed picture of Krishna on last year's Diwali card, chucked on top of a heap of discarded papers.

Shubha gripped the steering wheel hard.

The ashtray beside the telephone—had it been cleaned? Often, ever so often in these past few days, she had sat there smoking as she talked over the telephone. Suppose Ba were to ask why we needed an ashtray at all in our house? What then? Oh God! There was no time now to turn back to the house. She parked the car and went into the station.

The train arrived on time. The luggage was stacked into the car. Shubha slid behind the wheel and started the engine and Ba got in beside her. Inching her way through milling crowds, sounding the horn intermittently, slamming the brakes on at traffic lights, she drove homeward. The driving, the traffic and the tortuous progress, she had grown used to it all now and could manage mechanically.

Ba talked. As she talked, the fatigue of the journey was shot through with the lively satisfaction that lit her face. Crisply, rapidly, Ba went about recounting the little happenings and family gossip, as she always did. Like the clickety-clack of needles knitting all the inconsequential details into the common tale of the extended Indian family. Aunt, nephew, cousin, grandmother, crisscrossing relatives gathered together to celebrate or to mourn.

The car ran on. It had to run on. Ba's words flitted out of the window like dry leaves swept along by the afternoon breeze. Shubha was quiet. Her thoughts hovered round that ashtray near the telephone—cigarette ash wafting in the air.

Home at last. Pressing the horn twice to summon a servant, Shubha ran up the stairs, not even waiting for Ba to alight. She went straight to the telephone. No ashtray there. Damn it! She herself had put it away into the cupboard this morning.

Ba came in and headed straight for the photographs. Bapuji and Subodh smiled through the film of dust. Only four months after Shubha had stepped in as a bride, father and son had died together in a road accident.

A crystal bowl decked with fresh young blossoms had once dashed to the floor and shattered. Since then, like the myriad splinters of glass, were the moments of life: each to be picked up, one at a time, and one by one to be put away.

Ba carefully cleaned the photographs, knelt down and touched her head to the floor. Rising she turned to Shubha, and on a faintly reproachful note asked, "My dear, how did so much dust gather? Surely you remembered the fresh flowers and obeisance every day?"

One could make excuses—of a patient being ill, of visits to be paid. But words failed Shubha. She walked slowly out of the room.

Outside, she stood leaning against the rails of the balcony. Ba, she thought, must now be busy washing and bathing. At once she was seized with an irrepressible urge. The small space between thumb and finger throbbed palpably.

She went back to the room. Ba would take a long time in her bath. She pulled the packet out with an impatient hand and lit a cigarette, taking in the first few drags hungrily. Oh God. Just to quell the restless thirst of hours. . . .

One cigarette smoked, she lit another from its end. This too must be finished before Ba came out. She stood there and inhaled the smoke, deep and steady.

But how long can this go on? How long can the act be kept secret from her mother-in-law? There was the clinic, of course, where she could smoke. But Ba might just walk in there too, one day.

The sound of the bathroom door being unlatched broke her reverie. She flung the cigarette away, turned her head and peered. No, Ba was not yet back. She drew a long breath and sank down on the cane sofa.

Life. How it stretched interminably. How inexorably the seconds tick away. No might in the world can give them a shove and push them back. Time. . . .

A wave of exhaustion swept over her all at once. As if she had been plodding miles, carrying a heavy load. Now she only wanted to sit, just sit with a cigarette dangling from her listless hand.

"Don't you have to go to the clinic today?" Ba's voice reached out to her.

"I'm going," she answered, and snapped her purse shut. But she remained rooted to the sofa. The prospect of the clinic was depressing.

The faces that waited for her there would be dismal, every one of them, some bereft of all hope. To think of them was to enter that gray realm. "I cannot eat a morsel, doctor." "A fever of 100 degrees since yesterday." "The swellings on the feet have not gone down." Some throats riddled with swollen glands, some tumors destined to live or to die, a ceaseless tug-of-war and unending complaints.

She heaved a sigh and just as she was about to rise and leave, Ba came in. Seeing Shubha still sitting, she drew up the cane chair opposite and sat down.

"Shubha, the wedding was really great fun, very enjoyable. Oh dear, we—now let's see, how many years since I last saw a wedding? Your wedding, of course, and after that—oh well. But Mama was hurt that you did not attend. I explained to him of course. She is a doctor, I said. She has a commitment to her patients. Far be it from me to come in the way of her duty. What do you say? Isn't that so?"

An answer. One must say something now. Ba was waiting for a response. That is how it should be—some give-and-take, some conversation. Without these mundane exchanges, a home would freeze into one of those two dimensional stills. Her voice, pitched a shade too high, broke the lengthening pause. "How did Indu look as a bride? Was she dressed heavily for the occasion?"

"Yes indeed, dear. They had called in one of these makeup artists, you know. A full hundred rupees she charged! But Indu looked like a doll."

Ba pulled herself up a bit and continued, "You know Shubha, it really makes me laugh. These modern girls are all just dolls, mere dolls. Not a jot of idealism, noble thoughts or sensibilities."

Shubha gazed out in silence as the evening spread its shadow over the earth. She looked into the falling darkness.

"Come, now. You'll be late for work," Ba said. Shubha rose to her feet. Clutching the balustrade firmly in hand, she walked down the steps and out of the house. She started the car but after a moment switched off the engine. She would walk to the clinic today, she decided. It was only a short distance and she was in no mood to drive.

At the clinic, she found a large number of patients waiting for her. She took them all in at a glance. At the end of the line sat a man, neatly dressed, middle-aged. Their eyes met. An enigmatic smile played on his lips as he said, "I've been waiting for you for ever so long."

Shubha reacted with a start. It was not the words or voice so much, but the smile that was disquieting. A shiver of fear. As if this man could read her mind, as if he knew all, inside out.

She turned her eyes away in haste. She sat erect in her chair and answered, a trifle too loudly, a trifle too crisply, "Sorry, I have been delayed a bit."

One after another the patients came up to her. Some were advised to consult a specialist, for some an X-ray, for others merely an aspirin. It was all so routine. And the eyes of the man at the end of the queue somehow radiated strength to her— enhancing her capabilities, her insight, and her confidence. Yet there was that undercurrent of irritability, a weariness, an over-whelming desire just to let go!

She glanced at him. His smile hurt her, chased her about like some little whirligig, a sparkler that children light on fes-tival nights which scatters a shower of thrill and fear round and round in its zigzag trail.

Most of the patients had departed. It was his turn now— the last one. A cigarette. The urgent need to smoke welled up in her. Her fingers pulled out a cigarette from her purse. The man sprang up and lit it with his own lighter.

"Thank you."

He then sat down in the chair opposite her.

"Latika has been unwell since yesterday. Doctor, would you please come?"

His voice now struck dread, like his haunting smile. His words, so mildly spoken, were a confident invitation. Beneath the words lay the unspoken phrases: "I know. . . . I know it all. . . . Everything."

She stood up and said, "Yes, let's go. We shall watch for a day or two and then maybe call in a specialist."

He picked up Shubha's black bag, walked ahead to his car and held the door open for her. A moment's pause, then Shubha got into the front seat. He closed the door with care, walked round and got in beside her, behind the wheel.

Latika was of course not yet as well as she ought to be, but, even so, her condition did not quite merit a house call. Still, Shubha spent a long evening at their house. The long-ailing spinster and her bachelor brother together managed to keep the evening scintillating. She sat for a long time with the brother and sister, savoring the easy flow of conversation: the simple chatter that bounces off the walls of a house giving it the dimensions of a home. The fear of that smile had now vanished. Skeins of laughter and companionship spun a shimmering cocoon around her.

"Doctor, stay and eat with us," begged Latika. Shubha sprang up with a start and looked at her watch. Nine-thirty! Ba waited at home for her. She had returned.

"No thank you—it's late. Some other time." She stood up.

"I had no idea of your taste in these things. I have a number of imported brands—cigarettes as well as drinks," he said.

"Oh, no! It's only occasional. . . ." Murmuring, she crossed to the telphone, called the clinic, told the compounder to close for the day. She felt agitated, scared. She had lingered too long—the laughter, the jokes—for no good reason on earth. Life. She felt alive, and yet dreaded the very touch of life, afraid to come alive.

He drove her home in his car. Lifting her black bag in his hand, he offered to carry it upstairs. But she took it from him with a "No, thank you."

He did not move, but looked at her and said softly, "Will you not come again, unless my sister is ill? Won't you come over just to see us? We have really enjoyed your visit. You see, we are quite alone."

She could no longer stand there. Mumbling a formal "Yes, of course," she quickly climbed the steps.

A cloud of sweet incense hit her at the door. She entered the living room and saw the two photographs of Subodh and Bapuji draped with thick garlands of flowers. A bunch of incense sticks burned before them. The air hung heavy with the sweet scent. Ba sat on the floor facing the pictures, reciting the Gita.

Softly, Shubha crossed over to her room, put down her purse and taking the cigarette packet out, tucked it away into the cupboard. She washed her hands and face and rinsed her mouth with antiseptic. When she returned to the living room Ba had finished her recitation and was spooning the food onto the plates.

"I had to call on a patient. It got late," she said and sat down to eat.

Ba's hand stopped still in midair. Shubha jumped up and prostrated herself before Subodh's photograph. Subodh was smiling at her—a distant lifeless smile framed by fresh voluptuous blossoms.

As they ate, Ba began to talk again. Shubha barely heard her. Her thoughts, her being were still in Latika's house. The faint whiff of aftershave lotion, light laughter. "You see, we are quite alone." His words, his eyes. . . .

"We are quite alone." She heard the words distinctly again and looked up, startled. It was Ba talking to her.

"I told your Mama, 'Do not worry for us, brother. What if we are quite alone? I and my dear Shubha, we are quite apart from others.' "

Shubha looked down at her plate as she ate.

Ba spoke on: "Mama was all too full of praise, dear. 'Shubha is indeed a saint,' he said. 'Her life is like an incense stick. It burns itself to release its fragrance into the world.' "

Suddenly, Ba's voice ceased. Shubha looked up at her mother-in-law. A deep frown knitting her brow, Ba stared steadily into the corner opposite. She got up and walked over, and picked up something from the floor.

"Shubha, what is this?" Ba's voice cracked. Like hard dry earth. The barren sunbaked earth cracks, willy-nilly, along deep jagged fissures.

With thin trembling fingers Ba held up the burnt-out stub of a cigarette.

Translated from the original Gujarati
by Sima Sharma

Suniti Aphale ▰ *(Marathi)*

The Dolls

Shakun's perseverance was finally rewarded. She managed to make the doll stand, poised with an unbelievable balance; something she had been trying for so hard. At last she could relax. She leaned back in the chair and looked up at the clock. Eleven o'clock already! She had got up long before daybreak in order to give that one-and-a-half foot doll, the Bharatnatyam dancer, that stance: deeply curved at the waist in the pose of a peacock. It had taken so much of her time. Of course, it had been no ordinary task. To make the doll balance itself on one foot, and that, too, on the sole.

Having achieved that after so much toil, Shakun felt a thrill of satisfaction. She also realized how terribly tired she was—and very hungry.

It always happened that way. She would start making a doll and virtually fall into a trance. Slowly she began to be aware of things, one by one. The fresh milk was still lying uncovered in the outer room. Old Poonam had not yet appeared for work. Then she remembered it was Sunday. Poonam would take her own time. She desperately needed a cup of tea. But again she turned to the doll. Resolutely she began to attach the satin to the base of the board. "Kishorebhai is arriving tomorrow; how will this lady be complete by then?" she murmured.

Kishorebhai, of Bombay's *Dollsland,* wanted this doll urgently for one of his American customers. He was coming himself to Surat from Bombay in order to deliver it. She would be lucky if she could finish the job today, thought Shakun. Tomorrow, with the girls in the class around her, how would she possibly tackle it with any concentration?

But what she wanted now was tea. And there was no sign of old Poonam.

Suddenly the door opened. Instead of Poonam it was the neighbor, Savitaben. She had a plate in her hand, and on the plate were dhoklas.

"So this is what you've been busy with all morning?" Savitaben asked, looking first at the vessel of milk and then the doll. "That means you've had no tea or breakfast. See, I have cooked dhoklas, which you fancy so much."

"Just put one in my mouth," said Shakun as she got up to wash her hands all sticky with Stickfast. "I am so hungry."

Savitaben looked admiringly at the doll, then turned to Shakun pretending anger. "Shouldn't you feel hungry? Or do you feel it is wrong? How you neglect your health! Why don't you relax a little on a holiday?"

"I couldn't possibly!" Shakun exclaimed as she washed her hands. "Once these dolls are nearly finished they grab you round the throat like ghosts. They don't let you sleep, night after night. . . . But now I'm not going to accept such large orders. I have made up my mind. This doll is the last."

"You say that each time and yet go on accepting!"

"No, now this is really the last. These days I can hardly cope with it. You know how I have reduced the size of the class. Once there were fifty or sixty girls; now I have only five or six. I have crossed forty, you know. And that attack of flu has made me thoroughly weak. I get cramps in my hands and feet. . . . I just feel like lying down."

Shakun went on talking then suddenly stopped. . . . Why did she have to say all this to Savita? These days she found herself complaining to everybody about her health. The other day she had talked in the same vein even to the girls in her class. Why? All her life she had been bold and faced even her loneliness with confidence. Why did she have to seek these unnecessary props now?

Then she checked herself. "The dhoklas have puffed up nicely. . . . Did you use soda or baking powder?" she asked Savitaben.

But Savita was not listening. She was walking around the doll, scrutinizing it. Just then old Poonam arrived for work.

She, too, went straight to the doll. She smacked her lips with admiration and turned her gaze lovingly towards Shakun.

Shakun was pleased, and asked her to make three cups of tea. She also told her the menu: dal bhaat mathiya.

"I was at the doctor's just now," Poonam said. "There was a message for you. I still remember it. It's Nirupamaben's day for the injection. You are wanted in the hospital."

Shakun smiled. "Nirupama is nearing forty and she is still frightened of an injection. She can't do without me, can she!"

"And you go all the way every other day in this rain to that TB hospital!" Savita exclaimed, turning up her nose in disgust.

"Shouldn't I go, Savitaben? You tell me, who does Nirupama have except me?"

Poonam, her ears cocked, exclaimed from the kitchen, "They say you pay for the medicine, Shakunben. The doctor was asking, 'What relation is your Ben of Nirupama?'"

Why should the doctor ask? These must be her own inquiries, mused Shakun. "What relationship can there be? But one must do one's bit, surely?"

"Her husband, that Ramnik, what is he for, eh?" Savitaben asked.

"My dear, he has a lame daughter," Shakun expostulated, trying to protect Ramnik. "For her sake he has to go often to Mahalaxmi. . . ."

"And of course he leaves the younger one with you to look after! I must say, Shakunben, you do far too much for other people!" Savita again turned up her nose. She remembered how

Ramnik's younger daughter had once pushed her younger son down the stairs and how he had hurt his head. Since then, Savita had nursed a grudge against her.

Old Poonam, bringing tea, also took Savita's side. "Do even relatives do so much? I tell you, Savitaben, it's only because of our Ben that these people have a leg to stand on! Everyone says the same thing."

Shakun got up and began moving, just to stop the old woman from continuing to tell her what everybody was saying. "Ben, may I have your iron?" Savita asked. "Ours is always out of order these days."

As Shakun took out the iron from the cupboard, she wondered: were these dhoklas in return for the iron? And yet she had plied this cunning neighbor with all her tea! Aloud, she said, "Take it by all means. Anyway I don't like to use it these days. Keep it with you if you like. It will be convenient for doing your clothes." She turned to the old woman. "Make some nice tomato soup. It will be good for Niru. I shall take it with me."

"You are so late!" Nirupama almost shouted as soon as she saw Shakun. "The sister has already made two rounds. I asked her to wait only for your sake."

Shakun felt anger welling up inside her. Don't I have any work? Does she think I have so much spare time? And there was such a downpour just as I started from home! I am quite soaked. But she just doesn't see that. She is ungrateful and mean. I don't need to go to all this trouble and visit her!

"Why did you have to wait for me then?" Shakun asked.

"Whom should I wait for then?" Nirupama rejoined, but without any embarrassment.

Shakun felt deflated. True, she thought, neither Ramnik who calls himself her husband, nor Rasik, her son from the first marriage, ever turn up here. Who else should she wait for except me? She felt her anger had been unnecessary. This is the sort of persistent illness which could make people quite irritable a lot of the time.

So, quietly, Shakun put the thermos flask on the stool, straightened her sari, squeezed its edges and said, "I have brought you some tomato soup. Drink it hot. I have put some turmeric and jira in it. You like it don't you? I'll just go and get the sister."

Shakun could hardly walk with her wet sari sticking to her, but she went from ward to ward looking for the sister.

When Nirupama took the injection her darkened lips fluttered a little. She held her breath so that the veins under the skin of her throat grew big. She held Shakun's hand tightly. As she lent her support and helped her sit, Shakun thought again, really how badly she needs me!

The sister left. Nirupama lay for a long time with her eyes shut. It looked as if she was sleeping. Then, suddenly, she opened her eyes. "Come back again the day after tomorrow," she said. "And come a little early. Otherwise I have to keep waiting for you. Understand?"

There was neither helplessness nor urgency in her voice. It was an order. As always. Shakun also felt annoyed, as usual. Why did she have to visit this rude woman? She gets everything done as if by right! Why did I pamper her from the very beginning? It was my fault.

It had all begun during the time of Nirupama's first marriage when she was pregnant with Rasik. I went to the dispensary with her whenever she had to have some injections. And I have been doing that since. Why?

"Those earrings, are they new?" Nirupama suddenly asked Shakun but with seeming indifference.

"No, they are old. I haven't worn them for a long time. One of the pearls is missing in the ones I usually wear. I must get them repaired. I bought these years ago," Shakun said.

But why the need for her to offer this elaborate explanation? It would never satisfy Nirupama! She would continue to be suspicious.

"Many years? How many?" Nirupama asked.

"Oh, it must be about five."

Shakun was really annoyed. Nirupama always connected her old possession with Kantilal, Nirupama's first husband. She made similar minute inquiries about everything. As if, thought Shakun, before he married Nirupama, Kantilal had given me hundreds of saris and several sets of jewelry!

When Shakun had fallen in love with him in college, Kantilal had given her ordinary presents; even in later years it was always ordinary things. He was only a student at the time; he did not earn anything. And because he never worked at their shop, his father was always displeased with him. So Kantilal had very little money to spend. When his father died, Kantilal left college and started working at the shop. But lack of experience again made him lose money. In contrast, Shakun had begun making dolls even before she graduated. She used to spend more time in the doll-making class than with her books. She had even started selling these dolls very early. She had more money with her than Kanti. . . .

When she found Nirupama still staring at her earrings, Shakun flared up. "What are you staring at? I haven't stolen them, you know. I bought them myself."

Shakun never wasted an opportunity to cut Niru down to size in this fashion. She belonged to a caste slightly lower than Nirupama's. That was why Kanti's mother had stoutly opposed Shakun's marriage to him.

That was how Nirupama came to them as Kanti's wife. Although Shakun had not liked the idea, she had had to go with Kanti to his house to see the bride. At the very first meeting Nirupama had called her "Shakun" and she had called her "Niru." But that did not make up for the sneering way Nirupama had addressed her. "Did she think I was Kanti's maidservant? And that she herself was a great Queen?"

Then Kanti died. And it was Shakun's money which had helped set things right in his house. It was she who continued to support them. But from time to time she would make Niru realize that. . . ."

"When did Rasik see you last?" Niru's question awoke

Shakun from her reverie, making her feel restless again. The boy born of Niru's marriage to Kanti: he had started attending college now. Nirupama seems to take it for granted that he meets me! And she is questioning me!

"Why do you ask me? Ask him! He's your son, isn't he? Or is he mine?" said Shakun.

"He is my son of course. But he hasn't been here at all—while his mother has been in the hospital for a month. However, he visits you often. I am sure of it. Doesn't he?" Niru asked.

"Yes, of course, he visits me. He needs money, doesn't he? Hostel fees; college fees, books, exercise books. . . . And now he says he wants to have tuition. Says this is an important year from the point of view of admission to medical college. . . . I tell you frankly, Niru, the money from your shop which we deposited in the joint account finished a long time back. Also the money from the house. Many years ago. You know that, don't you? I don't have a money tree in my house!"

Nirupama just smiled a little cynically. "Why should you bother about whose money it is and where it comes from? This is an important year for me. You must give everything to him. It is, after all, a question of his life." Shakun was thoroughly irritated by her peremptory tone. "Do I have the sole monopoly of looking after all of you?" she shouted. "Am I the only one who is supposed to do this?"

"Don't get angry without reason. These days you get annoyed at the slightest pretext. If you won't do it who else will? Is there anyone, eh? . . . Since I got married again—to Ramnik—Rasik has been behaving as if he is demented. Now I realize that when I married again I lost my hold over my son. You could have given me a hint of this when I got married," Nirupama went on.

"Me? That's wonderful! All the advantages and disadvantages of a second marriage—you could have seen them. After all, Kanti was alive, even though he was bedridden, till Rasik was about nine years old. The boy must remember his father all the time. Rasik always was a pet of Kanti's. It must be hard for him to accept Ramnik as a father."

"Why should it be hard? He was not so small when I married. He was fifteen. But he has no understanding, I tell you. He speaks rudely to Ramnik, he beats up Ramnik's young daughter, he pinches and nags the lame girl. . . . Why? Why is he so vicious?"

"He must be taking it out on you for forgetting his lame father and making a new marriage. . . . Oh well, this is just my guess, you know. . . . Who shuld know better the turns and twists of his mind, you or me?"

Nirupama just turned her back to Shakun and began to mumble, "I feel drugged already. . . ."

Shakun cursed and got up. She washed the glass Niru had used in the nearby sink. She washed the thermos flask thoroughly.

As she left the hospital, she thought, how callous and evil-minded she is! Why do I take the trouble to visit her? And to think of wasting all that money saved for one's own old age on this arrogant woman! Was she herself so stupid and shameless? No, she wouldn't visit her anymore. Let her cry as much as she likes. What concern is it of mine?

As Shakun walked towards the bus stop she felt very depressed. She remembered how her father had often said, "Kanti is not a graduate like you. He has no heart in the business. You are good-looking. Besides, you are an only daughter. I can get a good husband for you. Don't have any truck with a vagabond like that boy." But she hadn't listened. Kanti was quite impressive to look at. What struck one was his aggressive, manly arrogance. A lock of hair always fell across his forehead. When he threw it back with a shake of the head and said something proudly, she did not have the strength to say no to him.

That is why when Kanti continued to visit her after he got married, she couldn't say no to whatever he proposed. Once, when she tried hard to break with him, he cried out angrily, "I know we didn't get married, but does that mean we have to finish with our love? If it's my mother and these orthodox relatives . . . I have no control over them you know. But what I have I am not going to give up! I'll continue to visit you. And you, too, must visit me!"

"But what about your wife? . . ." He reacted to those words only by tossing back that strand of hair as if to say he had given nothing less than an order!

She realized now how foolish she had been to respond like that to his male ego. She wondered too, how he could have talked so aggressively with her and yet been so different with his mother?

She also wondered sometimes if Kanti had not used his mother as a pretext for keeping her at arms length. . . . Kanti, too, had exploited her for serving his own ends.

Then, overnight, tragedy struck Kanti. A truck passed over his leg and he became lame. That was the time when Nirupama was pregnant with Rasik.

That meant Shakun had to try and nurse Kanti and somehow manage to look after both his mother and Niru at the same time.

Kanti's mother would call her endearingly "Ben," "daughter," etc., and flatter her into doing a lot of chores for her. And this was the woman who thought my caste was a low one!

Shakun poured money and hard work into putting Kanti's wrecked home into shape again. She sold the shop. Kanti was permanently bedridden. So it was Nirupama who would visit her and call her home.

Shakun first started visiting for Kanti's sake, and then continued for Nirupama's.

She had to accompany her to the dispensary from time to time for checkups. She had to look after her during her pregnancy, transporting her and bringing her home. All this was done only by her. How close Shakun had come to Niru in those days! But Niru didn't relent. Consciously, proudly, she would make Shakun do things for her.

Shakun approached the bus stop, filled once again with resentment against Nirupama.

She hadn't even remarked upon the quality of the soup. Then why did she drink it down? And what did she talk about anyway? Only about Rasik. As if there was nothing else in life!

Yes, but what else was there in her life besides Rasik? She had entered into a second marriage with Ramnik, but within a year it was evident to everyone that they didn't see eye to eye with each other.

And then there were the two girls from Ramnik's first marriage. One of them was lame, and the other very mischievous. Niru looked after both of them, but indifferently. In the last three years they had not taken to her nor she to them. Probably that was why Ramnik was sour with her.

Nirupama must have suffered because of all this. And Rasik too behaved as if he were her sworn enemy. He had insisted on moving to the hostel. Oh, I knew all this, thought Shakun, and yet I argued with Niru needlessly. . . .

It had stopped raining. The water which had collected in various corners began to flow quietly. As she skipped over the puddles Shakun realized that the air was colder. Did Nirupama wear a sweater or not? Did she have a sweater at all? Old Poonam had said that the doctor had asked for her to see him. She should have called on him. She could at least have felt under Niru's pillow and found out whether the doctor had given her any fresh prescriptions. Nirupama didn't talk about herself . . . she had an infinite capacity to suffer. It was not that Kanti was totally dependent on me while he was alive, Shakun recalled, and that therefore I had to look after his wife, too. Ultimately, one had to think of Nirupama as a human being and that, too, at a time when she was leaning on me—and only on me—for support. . . .

The bus which stood in front of her was not hers. She realized it was the one which would take her to Ramnik's house. Ramnik is terribly callous! Does he think his wife is dead? Can't he even visit her? He was pampering his first wife's daughters far too much. He had said last Thursday that he was going to Mahalaxmi; how was it then that he hadn't left his younger daughter with Shakun to look after? Was it because he didn't go after all? Or did he leave her with someone else? When he had first come from Nadiad to Surat it was Shakun who had helped him. She knew he came from her hometown. Who else did he have here who knew him that well? Has he now made friends with somebody who has agreed to look after the younger girl? Did that mean that he had no need for her, Shakun, any longer?

The thought left her suddenly unnerved. . . . How was it that she had not realized this before? She must meet Ramnik.

So, pushing aside people, seeing to her umbrella, her purse and the thermos flask, Shakun climbed onto the bus and stood holding the bar.

What a rush it was! Her knees began to ache. It would be three or four hours before she got home. That meant her wet clothes would dry on her body. She just couldn't cope with all this. These days she had no zest for anything. . . . But where could Ramnik have left the little girl? She had to find out. . . .

The bus was shaking gently as it sped along the road.

This Ramnik had come from Nadiad with his two daughters. A widower. He first came to her saying that he was from her town and that he had known her father. She had helped him find a house and a place for his shop and to set up everything else. He started a general store. It was she who had suggested that he should keep all the material needed for doll making in his store. That would do him good, she thought. . . . Ramnik was a persuasive man. He was full of sweet talk. He could win a stranger's heart in a minute. That was his nature. But Shakun had interpreted this differently. She had devoted herself to him so blindly that she never realized that it was Nirupama who had captured his heart.

Did he think of Nirupama even as he laughed and talked with her? Had he felt that he would not be able to manage with an unmarried girl who had money, was established in business like him, and was also good-looking? Perhaps he felt that only a woman like Nirupama, herself in need and in difficulty, would accept the impoverished and broken up life that he had to offer. That meant that the fact that she, Shakun, was secure in every way was a disadvantage compared with Nirupama's crumbling life!

Nirupama had come to stay in her flat. The money kept in their joint account from the sale of the shop after Kanti's death had begun to diminish. It was Nirupama herself who had said, "Now let us sell the house." Kanti's mother had objected, but after her death Nirupama sold the house anyway and moved in with Shakun. Then she had started sitting vacantly day and night saying, "Find a way for me to maintain myself." As if it was Shakun who had led her astray. "Find a way! . . ." She should have refused the responsibility of putting Nirupama on her own feet then and there. She should have done it firmly and with words of warning.

But Nirupama came as if she were totally dependent on her. She even had the temerity to ask Shakun, "These ten thousand rupees will be spent soon. Aren't you going to do anything else for the future?" It was as if looking after Niru was part of the job of looking after herself!

Nirupama was not even a matriculate. Where could she get a job? She was not ready to learn either. "Try to make dolls at home," she was told, but she showed no enthusiasm, no skill, no mental urgency for undertaking such a task. At that time Shakun had hundreds of girls in the class; she taught them in three batches. It was the heyday of her doll-making enterprise. If Niru had wanted she could have benefited. But she behaved as if it was Shakun who was the one in need. She just sat idly. It was Shakun who looked after Rasik also. Even that did not prod Nirupama into making any progress. She made a mess of all the dolls she made, and Shakun had to redo everything.

Shakun used to visit Ramnik's house fairly often. When he came in the morning he would collect orders from her girls; some students wanted tinsel, some fake jewelry, some velvet,

some saris, cloth, gems. . . . He would take down all the sizes,
the different silk threads, the various colors of hair, anklets,
etc., and bring them back in the afternoon. Then he would take
the next order, and similarly deliver it.

He too used to earn a lot. He used to laugh and talk and
make jokes. It was his habit to stand very close to you, almost
brushing you with his body. Soon Shakun found herself desir-
ing him. She would get a lot of orders for Ramnik from the girls.
Often they were unnecessary but profitable for Ramnik.

Ramnik was new in the business, and behaved as if he was
dependent on her. But within a few months he had made it on
his own. His shop grew along with his business. He engaged a
few helpers. He even bought a scooter.

At that time Shakun was so busy with her classes that she
never realized when Ramnik began to grow close to Nirupama.
Once, he dropped in on a holiday. When he found that Nirupama was out he lingered for a while. "What would you think if
Nirupama took care of my desolate life and my daughters?" he
asked all of a sudden. He didn't even notice that Shakun was
struck dumb. "Why don't you arrange the match? You do so
much for me. Do this, too. I shall no longer be a man without
someone to look after my needs!" He said this and went away.

What more did he find in Nirupama than in Shakun? Or
was it that he found so much in Shakun that he didn't dare
think of her as a wife? How did he find anything attractive at all
in Nirupama with her rapidly emaciating looks? Or was he
bothered only about getting "yes" for an answer?

In Kanti's case Shakun had been able to at least openly
curse his mother and cry. This time she couldn't even do that.
When it is your own foolishness that forces you to be unhappy,
you feel so guilty you cannot savor even that peculiar martyred
sense of happiness that lies within your unhappiness. That is
what had happened.

When Nirupama returned home she started grumbling.
"That Ramnik of yours is just chasing me. He stops me on the

road and doesn't stop talking. What kind of a man is he? I only ask because you know him better. And what is he thinking of? . . . If he is sure, try to sound him. Don't do anything permanently for me but do this at least. . . ."

There was nothing left for Shakun to do or not to do. The two of them arranged everything by themselves. So much so that neither of them realized how demoralized Shakun had been.

As Shakun entered the courtyard of Ramnik's house she found his younger daughter with a sling around her neck playing gilli-danda with her free hand. Shakun wanted to ask the girl what was ailing her now, but she only said, "Hello, Baby, why didn't you come to our house on Thursday?"

"I had gone to Bombay with Daddy," she said without looking at Shakun, and struck the gilli.

"Why did you take her, eh?" exclaimed Shakun as she walked into the house. Ramnik was fitting the elder girl with her new shoes and she was crying that they were too heavy.

When he saw Shakun, Ramnik tried to flash a hearty smile. But Shakun couldn't help noticing that his face was tired and he was perspiring. How thin Ramnik had grown these days!

"Why did you take Baby to Bombay on Thursday?"

"Oh, I just took her! How long can I bother you, Shakun? And since she pushed your Savitaben's boy down the stairs, I have felt very embarrassed. . . ."

"Oh, enough of Savitaben! Children are bound to behave like that," she said with relief. "I was wondering whether you left the girl with someone else. Do let her be with me, eh?" And then she wondered whether she was talking sense. Shouldn't she ask first about the girl's hand? "What scrape did she get into?"

"She fell from the mango tree yesterday. She has a double fracture. It's three hundred rupees gone in one day, Shakun. This one has new shoes. I spent more than seven hundred in Bombay alone. Even the shop was closed all of last week. And such a pile of expenses! Really, Shakun, I am trapped for good in all these affairs!"

"Well, that's what life is, isn't it? If you were going to get so fed up, you shouldn't have taken on new responsibilities as well!"

The dart hit home all right.

"I understand what you are saying, Shakun. But what can I do? I am broke. Niru is not the type of woman who can bear this state of things. She is quite capable of insulting me in the dispensary in front of others. How can I take the girls there? If only that so-called son of mine had offered to look after the girls, I could have paid her a visit. But he never turns up. I know you go and see her, Shakun, so I can leave everything to you and breathe freely." Ramnik tried to smile again. But he couldn't manage it and looked rather pitiable instead.

She ought to have considered Ramnik's point of view before flaring up, thought Shakun. Then she felt so bad for him that she almost wanted to put her arm around him and reassure him. She realized he could no longer smile spontaneously and brightly the way he used to. How attractive that smile had been!

Meanwhile, the lame girl had reached the door with difficulty and was calling Ramnik to come and see what she had achieved.

Shakun looked at the girl with her crippled legs, and the rest of the body growing. . . . She thought soon she would come of age. What about the daughters' marriages? And what would Ramnik do selling pots and pans? She was suddenly overwhelmed by pity. She felt she would like to help him.

"Had Rasik looked after the shop, do you think I would have lost so much of my earnings? But he just stays aloof. . . ."

By now Shakun was completely pacified. And as if she were unquestioningly on his side, she asked, "How is it that he never drops in here?"

"If he could do that, why would he have insisted to his mother that he stay in the hostel? He used to threaten her with suicide, you know, Shakun . . . I have heard it with my own ears. I tell you Shakun, he never liked our marriage. He considers me his enemy because I became his father and he considers his mother an enemy because she became my wife!"

Suddenly Shakun remembered Kanti after the accident and how Rasik would always be hovering around him. Kanti always used to tell him stories. The boy would feed him with the berries he had picked from the garden. "When I grow old I am going to be a doctor and give Papa a magic injection to make him well. . . . Then I shall race with him, Aunt Shakun!" he would tell her every time she met him.

Shakun wondered why she should blame Rasik for the way he was behaving.

"Actually, his mother should give him a good talking to," Ramnik said, "she has just become his slave. Nirupama never put her heart into my life. She has no affection for the girls. And that horrible cough of hers every night! I was a fool to marry again. . . ."

Shakun got up and said, "It was your decision to marry Nirupama. Yours alone. Now you can try to undo all the knots in your life. Don't rope me into it!"

And as though she was freeing herself from being sucked into a vortex, Shakun stalked out of the house.

By the time Shakun reached home it had become dark. Her sari had dried on her body. Her legs were cold and stiff like wood. She could hear them creaking. She was so tired that she began to feel feverish. She changed and rubbed a lot of balm into her feet. Then she covered herself with a sheet and sat on the divan. She didn't want to eat, and she felt like falling asleep where she was. That meant she wouldn't even have to go into the bedroom. She could just lie down here, looking at the dancing Bharatnatyam doll and think of how to dress and decorate her. She must finish it tomorrow. Kishorebhai would be coming to fetch it.

What would be the result of his divorce case, she wondered? Any woman who refused to live with such a nice man must be strange, indeed.

Shakun knew she liked Kishorebhai a lot. If only he had come into her life earlier, she could even have had an affair with him. The main thing was that he was not proud like Kanti nor childish like Ramnik. How serious he seemed!

He was going to like this doll immensely, she was sure. It had thoroughly tired her out. But how beautifully it stood! Kishorebhai had paid her only five hundred rupees for it. How much would he sell it for? He tried to find very big customers. She had supplied him with a lot of goods all these years. He must have earned a lot on the strength of her skill. But all that money went on that wife of his!

He didn't talk much, but once or twice he had let fall a remark that she was a spendthrift and that she grumbled when she didn't have money in hand. Did that mean he had exploited Shakun's art in order to keep his wife happy?

Suddenly she felt very angry with Kishorebhai. She began to be nagged by the thought that he paid her very little and made her toil only to suit his own ends.

But who had not exploited her? Kanti, Ramnik, even her neighbor, Savitaben! All of them were selfish. Shakun herself was foolish enough to have struggled unnecessarily for the sake of all of them!

No more of this toiling and struggling, she thought. She was dead tired. Now she would refuse everything. She would not do anything for other people.

Just as she was falling asleep, Shakun found Rasik standing in the doorway. It was Sunday. How was it she hadn't remembered he would be coming today?

"Come in. Why are you late?" she said, waking up.

He spoke stiffly. "I dropped in thrice. It's only now that I find you in." He pretended he was not really visiting her and, with his back towards her, started inspecting the doll.

"Fantastic!" He shook his head with such appreciation that she got up without meaning to.

How like Kanti he looks these days! The same height. The broad shoulders. He even had the same habit of proudly sweeping back that strand of ginger hair. Kanti, too, had known whatever there was to know about dolls. He was a true connoisseur. Rasik in front of her was a refreshing reminder of Kanti. . . .

"I really wonder how you managed to make her stand?" murmured Rasik.

"It was not so difficult. I first decided to make it like this, and then it was thrilling to make it stand. A real challenge!"

Whenever she used to make a really intricate doll, she would just have to take it to Kanti. If Kanti had been alive, life would have been so different. . . .

"You must have been paid quite a lot for it, eh?" Rasik asked.

This couldn't be Kanti's voice that talked about payment. This was Nirupama, the one who wanted to make others slave for her!

So Shakun replied rather curtly, "Yes, I was paid a lot, but that money is finished. What I paid for your books and exercise books came from that very amount."

She felt she would like to cover herself now with a counterpane and lie down. "Give me a crocin tablet from the cabinet. My body is aching."

Rasik gave her the tablet and brought her some water to drink. "Why do you go out in the rain?" he asked her, almost like a cross examiner.

"I had gone to see your mother," she retorted angrily. "Don't you ever go and visit her?"

"Will she be happy to see me?"

"Why not?"

"Huh! Well, I don't need that. And I don't have to visit other people to make myself happy."

Shakun suddenly felt depressed and terribly tired. Didn't this boy have a heart at all? She wondered if he knew about Kanti's relationship with her. Did he feel she had been devoted to his father without even being his wife, and was that why he had respect for her?

"Don't just talk and waste my time," he said. "What about giving me some money? I must join the class tomorrow. It's the last day. If I don't pay the fees, they will admit someone else."

With each word he spoke Shakun began to fume more and more. He didn't even talk with humility. It was as if she was the one in need, not he!

She cut him short. "I can't afford the expense of your class. I am already paying for the hostel, your mess, the college fees, books, exercise books . . . and now the class! I can't manage it any longer. I have only a few girls in the doll-making class. I am going to stop accepting big orders. This is the last one. I am tired."

"But this is an important year. It's a question of life and death for me."

"How long should I try and prop up other people's lives, eh? . . . I really can't cope with these affairs, believe me!"

Suddenly there were footsteps outside the door. Kishorebhai had arrived. Before she could see his face, she saw the big suitcase in his hand. Did that mean he was going to spend the night here? This had never happened before. He always came in the morning and left by the evening.

Then Shakun remembered his divorce case and a strange idea came to her. She should have been wearing a better sari. And when she had returned home, she had not even combed her hair properly or powdered her face!

She began to feel very awkward about Rasik and Kishorebhai being with her at the same time. She wanted to get rid of Rasik. "There must be some sweets in the kitchen cupboard," she said to him. "Have them if you want and go. It will soon start raining again."

"No, I don't want anything." Rasik pushed back his strand of hair and said roughly, "Just keep the money ready. I shall be back tomorrow afternoon." His eyes glowed angrily like cinders as he turned and left.

Shakun felt as if there had been a sudden fire and the smoke was smothering her.

Crestfallen, she turned to Kishorebhai, told him to have a seat and went to prepare tea.

"Aren't you well? You look so worn out!" Kishorebhai called out as he lit a cigarette.

"Oh, I am all right," she said, "I just got caught in the rain!"

Kishorebhai followed her in. "I have brought some sweets for you. You like them don't you?"

"What is the outcome of the case?" she asked eagerly.

"Oh, that was over a long time back. These are in celebration of my daughter's engagement. It took place just the other day."

"Congratulations," she said hurriedly, "but how is it that you came today? Weren't you going to come tomorrow? The doll still needs a little work on it."

"Don't let it weigh on your mind that I am here a day earlier. The doll is first-rate. Really excellent. Whatever little decoration is left I'll do myself tomorrow. I came today because I have found a French customer. He wants to get this picture of a garba dance worked into dolls. He wants it within a week. That's why I rushed to you."

So, he too had hurried only because of his need!

As she strained the tea, Shakun looked at the picture Kishorebhai had placed in front of her. She could visualize the dolls that would emerge from the picture.

"It will be a nice thing, you know!" she said off her guard.

"I knew you would like it!" he said, slowly drinking his tea. She became alert again.

Her dolls were in great demand in his shop in Bombay. Foreigners, especially, flocked to the shop. Shakun knew he must be earning a lot of money from their orders. Again, she was needled by the suspicion that she herself was being paid very little for her work.

"It's work which calls for a lot of tenacity," she said quietly just to get an inkling of what he had in mind.

"Well, I've only got eight days to go. You have to do the scene in a week's time. I can stay here and help you with whatever you want. I had planned to stay anyway, and I have brought these ready-made hands, legs, and faces with me. If you just use them and are quick enough. . . ."

He finished his tea quickly and opened his suitcase. He drew out box after box and opened them. There were hands, legs, bodies and faces.

With every box that was opened Shakun would say, "No, this is no use."

After opening the last box Kishorebhai said with some asperity, "Now look, do you fancy these legs at least?"

She laughed cynically. "Well, well, look at the words you are using! You are a born merchant! You don't have the heart or eye of an artist."

"You have told me that often enough before," Kishorebhai returned peevishly, "but I thought you could make do with these."

"That's just it! It's one thing to make do and another to put your life and soul into it. If you wanted just a makeshift job, there are many in Bombay who could have done that."

"Perhaps you are right! I was stupid to come rushing here to you!" he said with deliberate callousness. But he could not hide his disappointment. "Are you saying 'no' just like that?" He thrust his hand into the box again and frisked through more specimens of feet. "There are so many patterns here. Besides, they are of export quality. . . ."

"Why can't you understand?" she said sticking determinedly to her position. "If it has to be the garba dance, it will require at least eight cowherds and milkmaids, eh? The milkmaids' petticoats you will have to keep short. That means more than half the calf will be bare. Both the feet will be bare. And those, too, must be dancing as to a rhythm, isn't that so? . . . Even the cowherds will be dancing. So these flat feet won't be of any use. All of them will be dancing to rhythm, in style. Some will be standing on their soles. At least one or two milkmaids will have their legs in the air, don't you think?"

"Yes, of course!" Kishorebhai said, nodding his head appreciatively.

Shakun felt all the more elated and continued, "So these stock feet will be no use. They will look quite shapeless. I shall have to make them myself. . . ."

"I know I can depend on you entirely," Kishorebhai said eagerly, "I wonder how you manage all these subtleties. . . ."

"Yes, but what do you care about that?" Shakun flared up suddenly. "You'll make a lot of money out of it!"

Shakun refused to be exploited again. She was clear now about what she wanted. "I want fifteen hundred for this garba dance," she said. Not a line stirred on Kishorebhai's face. She became all the more alert. "And all the silk, clothes and gems . . . you'll have to bear the expenses. It's all very expensive these days. One can hardly afford it."

"Why are you arguing about money, eh?" Kishorebhai pacified her, sidetracking from the main point. "What matters is whether you can finish the job in time. That Frenchman is returning next week. That means you'll have to make these eight dolls in four days. Krishna is the ninth. Two more days to make them stand, and one day for decorating. I shall stay and help you. Ask your girl students to help you also."

Shakun seethed with anger. He was just ordering her about. The man was using her art for his own profit.

"I have to get into the mood, don't I? You can't force me to work like this!" she exclaimed sharply. Then she turned her back towards him and started washing the cups and saucers. Kishorebhai begged her, "Don't be like that! I know you'll get into the mood. It's such a challenge for your art. You'll make such beautiful dolls that people will just look at them in amazement. They will think that any moment the dance will begin and Krishna's flute will start playing. . . ."

Shakun suddenly stopped washing and scrubbing. Her hands started twitching. She was seized with an urge to start making the dolls that very moment. She realized, however, that Kishorebhai had said all that with a deliberate purpose. He wanted to get her to commit herself.

She said obstinately, "No. These days I can't bear all this rush and tension. I can't keep late nights. I get tired easily."

"Shakun, I came here with great hopes, you know," Kishorebhai pleaded. "This customer is really big. After him, we are likely to get many more from the French Embassy. This divorce case has left me completely bankrupt. I need money badly. I can't sleep these days because of money worries. I want some money for my daughter's wedding. And you, too, must be needing money? Come on, think about it."

So he wants me to confess I need money only because he himself is in need of money! Shakun cursed him silently.

"Come, let us dine out and see a film."

"No," she said peevishly, wanting to refuse everything. "You go if you want to. I am not hungry. I am feeling feverish. A film means keeping a late night. I can't bear it these days. You go, and take this duplicate latchkey with you. Then you won't disturb me at night."

Kishorebhai quietly picked up the key and left.

Perhaps she had been unnecessarily brusque speaking to him, thought Shakun. After all, it was because of him that she had earned thousands of rupees all these years. It was a business for him. He had to make a profit. Discovering customers among foreigners, negotiating with them, selling, holding exhibitions of dolls in the big cities, didn't he manage all this by himself? And, besides, he was such a thorough gentleman in his dealings. She should have talked to him more politely. She should have cooked some food for him. . . . After his wife left him he's probably never had a nice meal to eat.

Shakun rushed onto the balcony to call him, but he had already gone.

The clouds had sped away in the sky and there was bright moonlight. She could have spent a good evening with Kishorebhai. Was there something more behind his planning to go to a film? And his coming here to stay, what did that suggest?

Why did she have to block off what she wanted most and then prick up her ears when she thought she heard a footfall?

Shakun lay sleepless for a long time. When Kishorebhai returned very late, she was still awake, only pretending to be asleep. Then the door of the bathroom opened and closed. There was the sound of the chaddar being spread on the divan . . . then darkness. Suddenly she was very angry with Kishorebhai. Then she just sighed and tried to sleep.

When she got up it was well past morning. The milk had arrived and Kishorebhai himself had put the water to boil for making tea.

When he saw she was up, he put some more water into the pot and said, "Today, let me make your tea for you! How are you feeling?"

His question suddenly reminded her of her aching body of yesterday. But now, after a long rest, she was feeling very fresh. "Fine," she said, and then went and brushed her teeth.

"Why did you have to make the tea?" she said later, being a bit formal. "I would have made it myself." But when she drank it she felt such pleasure thinking he had made it for her with all that affection.

"Which film did you see?" she asked.

"Oh, no! I didn't see a film. I was in no mood. . . . Money worries. Business is not what it used to be. There is a lot of competition in Bombay. This court case was such a waste of time for me . . . and now that I have a big customer, I am going to lose him." Kishorebhai got up as if he were in a daze and asked, "Didn't you have a couple of girl students who were being trained by you? When I was here last they used to make very good dolls. That fair-complexioned one—rather fat—I think her name was Jyoti. . . ."

Shakun was slightly shocked. "She got married. She lives in Dahanu now."

"There were a couple more. . . . If you tell them to help

you, they won't say no. Now that I am going out, I'll make inquiries and see if I can get someone. I will eat out. That other doll . . . I hope it will be finished by the evening. I shall return to Bombay today. Let this latchkey stay with me. If you are resting in the afternoon, I won't have to disturb you . . . I'll see if I can get some help in town . . . can't let go of such a big customer, you know. . . ."

Shakun began to shake with anger. Was he now going to look for someone else? Was he also going to depend on some other woman to help put his life in order?

No, she wouldn't let him do that. She felt like crying out. She wanted to hold Kishorebhai rooted to the spot with all the strength in her hands. It was not that she wanted him so much but that she wanted him to go on depending on her. . . . She wanted that very much . . . to help others had been the mainstay of her life.

She opened her lips to speak to Kishorebhai. But he was not there. The door was shut.

Shakun sat still, feeling helpless. Today it was Kishorebhai who was freeing himself of his dependence on her. Tomorrow it could be Rasik, Ramnik, or Nirupama. . . . She thought her very roots were being pulled out.

She stood up like one possessed and left her house.

She went and saw Rasik first. She gave him all the money he required and then she finished with the doctor, with Nirupama and the medicines. Then she stopped her rickshaw at the door of Ramnik's house, thrust a lot of banknotes into his hand and made him open his shop. She selected some things, shoved a number of them in her bag and rushed to three or four of her students to ask them to see her at her house as soon as possible. Then she hurried home.

Without even eating anything, she sat down with her doll-making things.

Kishorebhai returned sometime in the afternoon. As soon as he saw Shakun busy with her dolls his face lit up with satisfaction.

She was surrounded by five or six girls, all absorbed in making the dolls. Two cowherds and one milkmaid were almost ready. One cowherd was in her hand.

"Bravo!" he said, and there was a hint of tears in his eyes. Then he swallowed and murmured, "I knew you wouldn't say no. I am depending entirely on you, Shakun! It is only because of you . . ."

He didn't say anything more. But Shakun understood. It was as if she had been waiting for this. Then, as she looked at him, she thought, how white his hair has turned . . . and how weak he looks! . . . This job will put an end to some of his worries at least. . . .

Then she said, "Don't worry. They will be ready in six days. That's the time you've got, eh? First I thought I wouldn't be able to manage. But, you know, I have spent my whole life making these dolls stand. My life depends so much on them. Now I feel if I deny them an existence life itself will collapse. . . .

"That's the only reason . . ."

And she went on sewing the folds without bothering whether the needle would hurt her.

Translated from the original Marathi
by Dnyaneshwar Nadkarni

Mrinal Pande ━━ *(Hindi)*

Tragedy, in a Minor Key

Kicked open the door. Lying inside was a letter superscribed with a fine, spidery script. The handwriting could only be Ma's. The last part of Ma's letters always effervesced up to the place which bore the legend: No enclosures allowed.

I threw the books on the table, and collapsed on the bed like a felled tree. Theatricality certainly has some elements which take the edge off problems. Even if only for a short while. This tired town of lawyers and professors becomes quite unbearable otherwise in these dusty months of February and March when anxiety and fear fill the air.

Hai exams! *exams!* I sang lustily. Outside my window the Gulmohar and silk cotton trees were a distracting eyeful, bursting with color in spite of everything. One look and your dread disappeared; your heart began to pull you one way and your feet another. Hai for a Man! For a Man! For a *Man!* I sang and my humor improved. Propping my legs up on the wall I tapped my lovely roughened feet in time, chanting my little rhyme. I opened the letter. Loads of news in Ma's familiar, breathless, and confusing style; news from here, there and everywhere, coming to rest at one point—I *hope* you've booked yourself a seat on the train for coming home in the vacations. I *hope* you're being careful about your diet. I hope you're paying attention to your studies at least this time—I hope! I hope! I hope! I crumpled up the letter into a ball and tossed it aside and picked up a mirror. I *hope!* I stuck out my tongue. If you are in a temper, it is very gratifying to look sympathetically at your face in the mirror. There is always something very reassuring about your image sticking its tongue out at you. Such unending affection and tolerance towards yourself renews your confidence in life despite everything.

Tong—Tong—Tong! goes the bell for lunch with its green metallic, sound. . . . The brass plate has formed many small, black pits like pimples where the wooden hammer strikes it. Come! Come! Come! An anxiety grips me just as it does the moment I reach home. Why is it that back home everything is so familiar and easy and overflowing with injunctions to relax, and yet, once there, every issue which seems so personal and manageable here, begins to rise and spread like a pall of smoke choking all of us? What is it? How is it? Is it because parents seem to want to strip the layers of your very skin, to enter your very insides; to poke, poke and poke until nothing about you is hidden from them? I hope, I hope, I hope! And as if this were not bad enough, I often suspect that, if they could, our parents would want even your dreams to become their property.

I fill a glass of water from the surahi and wave it in the air. A toast to all the departed optimists of the world! "Dear brothers and sisters," I want to say, "in spite of my best efforts, my will to fight is ebbing dangerously." I toss the toast out of the window. The patch of water looks like the subcontinent of Africa, drying slowly in the sun. The second bell for lunch is ringing. The calendar on the wall opposite flutters in the breeze. The wall bears a half-moon where the metallic edges rub against it every day. The abrasions remind me of a scraped elbow. In the beginning when we began to clash with Ma and Babu, it was Ma who was badly shaken, more so than Babu. One hardly knew when the soft acerbity of our exchanges and digs would turn into something else and, as the seriousness of accusations grew, the bitterness of the rejoinders began to snowball. "A melon takes color after seeing other melons," Babu would say. Chhota and I were the proverbial melons which inevitably got slashed whether they fell on the knife or vice versa.

Kalindi—Meena—Swapna—Vasanti—the whole flock is moving towards the dining hall, issuing peal upon peal of meaningless laughter. They are like smooth, glazed clay pots that no liquid can touch; dark blankets that no dye can stain. Their feelings never affect their stomachs. Even after the bitterest of political arguments, or a shockingly bad exam, they think nothing of demanding an extra sprinkle of sugar on their bowl of yogurt or chillies with their dal. Good-tempered, insensitive, passionless sheep, beloved of parents, perpetual gladdeners of hearts, ideal bearers of children, ever wide-hipped and wide-eyed. Feeling much better after venting my spleen, I was humming under my breath when I noticed Kishwar leaning against the door. "You look very cheerful, what's the matter!" Death and Kishwar were notorious for arriving without knocking, so I was not too surprised. A flowery housecoat wrapped around her ample bosom, a colored towel on her freshly washed head like a stupa—she stood there like an outsize question mark.

"Any special news?" Actually poor Kishwar did not merit the dubious reputation of a Wicked-Wormer-out-of-Secrets. She's basically quite nice and I have nothing against her, except her excrutiatingly filthy personal habits. Her window sill is always overflowing with open, fungoid bottles of pickles and jam. Her toothbrush resembles a shoe brush and if you ever spot her bra-strap peeping from under her blouse you almost puke. . . .

I sighed and put away my thoughts and got up on my elbow. I tried indifference: "Nothing, well, just generally . . ." But Kishwar did not budge. She stood there surveying the room with her cat's eyes. I speculated she would definitely touch me for something. She's famous in the hostel for borrowing and never returning things. "Are these chappals new?" She rudely thrust her painted hooves into my slippers. The nail varnish, I knew, was borrowed from Kalindi.

"Yes," I kept my voice carefully neutral.

"They're nice," she said, wriggling her toes, and pushed them away. "We're going to a movie. Want to come?" She started picking her teeth with her comb. "You're going home for the hols, aren't you?"

"Yes."

"Then come along. This film won't reach your home for another year at least!"

"I'll see," I said, and made an unsuccessful attempt at sounding bored. "Which one is it?"

She named a much talked-about movie full of suspense and violence.

"Tickets?"

"We'll manage," she shrugged indifferently. Her father was somebody important in the police and had been posted here at some stage. In some things his name still carried a lot of weight; not much, but in cinema halls, provision stores, and the like it did help. The old, ill-tempered gate-keeper of the town's best cinema hall called her 'Baby' and would guide us politely to our seats in the dark even if we were late. "Well! Let me know before noon—we'll be going at 12:30." She turned. As I watched her go, I felt like calling out to her and saying, "Dear Kishwar, please stay, talk to me for some time about anything, anywhere, save me from this loneliness, save me from myself, my friend! Suddenly, I was seized with laughter. I got up and put on my chappals, took them off and lay down again. I knew I would not go to the movie, and so did they. Why bother then, with these futile exchanges? I tried to concentrate on the ceiling now and to feel suitably sad again.

On a corner of the ceiling a spider was speedily spinning a web, running about furiously on its unbearably thin legs. I began to chew my nails. Last year, in spite of my parents' willing self-deception, my performance in the exams had been absolutely hopeless. In particular, I had messed up the world history paper. To tell you the truth, I could not stand the sight of Saxena who lectured us on world history. He may have been a bright student in his time but he had eventually got into teaching because of a somewhat ill-timed sentimentality. Most of his contemporaries were, by now, important bureaucrats in high places or corporate tycoons swishing about in air-conditioned cars, smoking Havanas. And all of this while he kept losing his hair and his temper as he repeated endlessly the tedious accounts of the Napoleonic wars in English. There were bad vibes between him and me from the very first day. Well actually, to let you into a secret, he reminded me strongly of K. Chacha, a dear, devoted friend of my parents. He had the same sharp, beaky nose and square jaw, the same affected jaunty walk and nasal speech. You're probably wondering what K. Chacha is like: you'll get a fair idea if you consider the compere on radio who presents "Phulwari" (a program for children). He's called Bade Bhaiya (Big Brother). You must've noticed how he sidelines the kids constantly and cracks unbearable jokes in a lisping childlike voice and then goes on to explain them! Well, that's K. Chacha all over!

"After all, we are from the older generation." No sooner had he uttered these words that our hackles began to rise. He was a great favorite of Ma's because he unfailingly supported her familial sermons. Also, in matters of food, his taste buds were supposed to be exceptionally sensitive. He could always tell when the servants had made the tea and when Ma had made it. "Houses are many, but a home can only be created by the lady of the house," he would say, and immediately propose that Ma had better teach me all these fine arts, "because you can't run a good house by reading G. B. Shaw and T. S. Eliot, especially if you are a girl." Got me? He was also a favorite of Babu's as he could hold forth at length about the debasement of values among the young in society with an occasional reference to Gandhism thrown in for good measure. In this triangular dramatic plot involving Ma, Babu, and K. Chacha, our presence (i.e. that of the brothers and sisters), was purely incidental. If you know what I mean.

"You can brand me a traditionalist," Ma would begin and K. Chacha would jump up saying: "Bhabhi, you are not using the right words. What you call being a traditionalist I'd term as being respectable, civilized. Now, since respectability cuts through time and class, nobody can get away from it by saying we belong to the new generation and your rules of behavior and manners are not applicable to us. What do you say—Young Rebels?" His obscenely adenoidal curiosity fattened like a leech on our presence. "Prove me wrong, if you can," he would wink at Babu and goad us further with a hostile laugh. "Come and sit with us a while, we would also like to have the opinion of the so-called younger generation. I hear you've become quite a radical, young man." I'd watch Bhaiya's tightening jaw and my stomach would contract. We tried our best, though, and the moment the chachas and mausis arrived, we would burrow into the remotest corners of the house. Nonetheless, loud snatches of their conversations followed us into our hideouts. We heard about Life and Sacrifice, the World and Society, the Need to Respect Elders and alas, the Decline in Manners! As if our parents didn't sermonize enough, God sent us all those relatives each week.

In this town of high fences and low vitality, our Malini Mausi lived in one of the old-style colonial bungalows with large brown gates and an equally large, unkempt, brown garden. As you entered the semidarkness of her house, the smell of fading distemper, slowly decaying wood, and dust would assail your nostrils as though you'd entered a dungeon. Sharp-tongued, Malini Mausi was an ever-suspicious, high-strung individual who seemed to nurse an anger and a bitter resentment against everyone like a secret deep inside her. Quite the opposite of our simple, pious and good-natured Ma. Her irritability and her nervous, halting mannerisms mirrored the agony of ill-used *womanhood* humiliated for centuries and then left to dry out. The events of her meteorically brilliant past had been narrated to us by Ma at least a hundred times. How her beauty and multifarious talents had dissolved into nothingness in this small town in the service of a narrow-minded, illiberal family of the most conservative sort . . . we heard how there had been a fifteen-minute ovation after her name was announced at the convocation, how everybody who knew her swore by her beauty. . . . But ever since we could remember, Malini Mausi had been like a tightly shut door which admitted, with an irritable creaking, only those who were her own flesh and blood. Our well-meaning and ever-optimistic Ma was one of those; but once in that house, the dark shadow of frustration and pain seemed to touch her also. "How different she was once . . . and look what she has become now . . . poor thing!" she would sigh.

A false start in her life under a harsh mother-in-law never let Malini Mausi regain her momentum even after the lady's death. Or maybe the mother-in-law was just an excuse. This mysterious Queen of Tragedies, our Malini Mausi, bore the heavy weight of Tragic Womanhood almost lovingly. When you visited her or when she came over, you could hear her complaining constantly in her high-pitched voice. All her pronouncements swung between an acute hatred of her femininity and a black self-pity. Any whiff of the masculine world, whether it was tobacco smoke, a vulgar joke, or loud laughter, would cause her acute agitation and she would sit full of hatred, ticking like an old clock for hours. Complaints were the refrain of her tragic song whether they were about the indifference and expensive habits of her sons, her husband's dull job that kept them permanently in a small town, or the increasing insolence of her old servants. Photographs in Ma's old albums showed her as a slender, pale, ethereal beauty, but now that beauty had disappeared amidst rolls of soft flesh. Okay, okay, I agree our own Ma was no New York fashion model either. But there was something so comfortingly maternal in her soft cushion-like fleshiness, redolent of mother's milk and sleep-evoking laps. Malini Mausi's fat was of a sour yeasty kind which is born of dark corners and tightly sealed containers, pungent and unhealthy. Mysterious female ailments were forever breaking her back and splitting her head with strange aches. Her embraces reeked of medicines and loneliness. But, to tell you the truth, in spite of all this, there was something very sad and touching about her. Perhaps it was the wordless pain of a creature who fights valiantly in the face of unjust circumstances, refusing to surrender to the forces of loneliness, of annihilation. In her final defeat all of us were somehow diminished.

By comparison, Chhoti Mausi's personality was far simpler. Where Malini Mausi took up the bitter challenge of resisting her circumstances, Shalini Mausi had surrendered to life and slipped unprotestingly into her permanent role of a child bride almost thankfully. Her joys, her petulance, and her speech were all childish and frivolous. She argued with her little son in English after which she either cried or made extravagant displays of affection. Her ambitions were limited to having a household full of imported gadgets and raising her young son to become an important officer. Her troubles, therefore, were also in a minor key: the maid not arriving on time, a pickle rendered inedible because of mold, or her son getting poor grades in the monthly exam. Ever-timid and always grateful, she filled that void in our Ma's life which we, her children, had created as we drifted away from her. The crumbling wall of Ma's dreams had once again begun to draw strength from this childish support. Or was it because we selfishly wished to believe that this was so?

My mouth grew bitter. I jumped up and thrust my feet into my chappals and started walking towards Pushy's room. Pushy is short for Pushpinder. A lusty Punjabi, overflowing with a zest for life, Pushy Grewal, the Sikh chick, had a slightly nasal voice and her pidgin English was proof of her schooling in Indian English convents. Her uncomplicated world was like a featureless expanse of green grass. It had no contours, no sharp-

edged rocks, no tricky ditches. She took an extraordinary interest in everything ordinary. Spicy chaat and gravy with lots of
ghee. Lata Mangeshkar's music, pulpy romances and the he-
man of the Indian screen, Amitabh Bachchan: she would die a
hundred deaths for any of these. Of course what with her hefty
frame and booming voice, you could hardly expect a less extravagant display of feeling.

"Oy Pushy!" I called, in nasal tones, leaning my torso over
the edge of the bannisters. No answer. I looked around. Next to
Pushy's room was Suruchi Asthana's room, austere, orderly,
and with just the right air of martyrdom to suit its mistress.

"She's gone out," said Suruchi's reedy, tired voice. There
was something in the good taste of Miss Good Taste which
brought out a vulgar streak in me. My crude display of disappointment caused Suruchi's respectable nostrils to contract; but
then she smiled her small, dusty, do-gooder smile. "Come in for
a while today, won't you?" I had to sit perforce. Suruchi is the
young replica of the average middle-class Indian mother like
Shalini Mausi. Ineffectual, ever conscious of propriety and forever grateful, she clears her exams with a middling 2nd division
every year. Her wardrobe is always in order, her clothes neatly
ironed and her hair well oiled. She is religious too. A portrait of
the goddess-astride-a-tiger-or-a-swan and a squatting idol are
affixed to her shelf where the row of bound books ends. There
is an offering of a flower and a burnt-out remnant of an incense
stick at their feet. Really, this girl is so transparent in her
holiness that looking at her, I always end up looking almost
through her into her future and, believe me, that is as bland and
smooth as her present. I can imagine her in her house ten years
from now, in a distant town with an Engineer/Doctor/Officer for
a husband. Beyond the splendor of her dowry furniture, her
polished bronzes and Ikebana bowls, the idols of her family
gods will be sitting in somnolent silence, dimly lit by an oil
lamp. I give noncommittal replies to her sleepy queries and take
my leave. "I have to pack you see . . . OK. Should I bring you
something when I come back? Think about it. Yeah. OK. Bye."

Exit into the wings, retouch makeup. Plays a role well, this girl! Thank you, thank you, thank you all.

"Have you eaten?" Nirmalaji pauses on the steps. She's the most respected, elderly, research scholar in the hostel. She's a young widow. But much older than everybody else here: sober, self-possessed and introspective. Her introversion does not rest on an irritable intolerance like Malini Mausi's. There is a calm in her, an inner stillness which holds, even though there is nothing exceptional about her face and form. And if the word 'respect' had not been vitiated for me by having so many sundry blockheads lumped under it, I would say I respected her.

"Have you eaten?" she repeats. Professional ham that I am, I cannot hedge in the face of this calm inquiry. "No," I say. Then suddenly, I can't resist a shot at Drama: "There's pumpkin on the menu today," (Clutching my stomach in a puking stance, tongue hanging out, eyes rolling.) "It aggravates my G-Ass-Ah!"

A hint of laughter crosses Nirmalaji's steady, brown eyes. "Look here Sudha, stop clowning, you've got to eat what's cooked. I've noticed whenever it's close to exam time you go all strange, you just hang around the whole day and crib. Just look at yourself. Come on, get up." There she goes, Christ's Aunt! Dadhichi's descendant! Gandhi's disciple! I know I'll go now. I'm the only bloody fool who has to obey every elder everywhere. I drag myself to the doors of the dining hall. Volumes of chatter float on the heat and the smell of food is all around. Most people are gulping the meal down with a fierce concentration, and others talking continuously. Every table is spattered with dal and yogurt. The chapattis are hard and the dal cold. "Should we warm it up for you?" the well-meaning serving girls ask. "No," I reply. I know if she goes back to the kitchen to reheat the bowl of dal she'll have to listen to the cook grumbling, and at the end of half an hour, will return with a bowl of lukewarm dal laced with ash. The lumpy pieces of pumpkin are smothered in chillies. I swallow the last mouthful and push the plate away.

Even so, this food doesn't taste so bad. At home, the food may be a hundred times better, but the moment Ma starts flapping around our chairs, the taste vanishes. Listening to her, one would think that food is a miracle cure for all ills. "Your face looks tired, it must be Vitamin B deficiency, have some more yogurt and a chapatti with extra ghee." "Didn't sleep well last night? The food must have been too heavy, I'll cook you something light today." "Don't feel like studying? A small dose of chyawanprash." No one bothers to ask what they should, and a thousand bits of advice are offered for what is none of anybody's business.

The sky overhead balloons like a canopy of dust, but beneath that the March blooms are a riot of color! Between the dust and the blooms stands our gray and black dining hall where a middle-class ritual is taking place. Gravies are being warmed on demand, pickles and brimming bowls of ghee-from-home are being shared, chapattis are being thrown to the dogs hanging about, sorrow and sympathy are being expressed over overweight figures. Grass, stones, food, and a slimy, oozing love. Ah! Suddenly, there's no bloody sense in life. Is there any sense in anything?

"What have you decided about coming along?" Kishwar, decently clad now, is drying her thick hair in the sun. "Where?" For a moment I don't understand the context. My eyes are blinded by the sun and the bright color of the flowers overflows and drips into my cheeks.

"Yar! The movie, where else?" She lowers her tone confidentially. "Or did you have some other program." Her sly innuendo is like a douche of cold water on my overflowing spirits. "No. Not today." "Well remember, not today means not at all. Mark that my dear 'cause tomorrow it's 'Homeward Bound.'" She hums and moves away. Not that she really expected me to come. I'm not one of her claustrophobically close friends in the hostel—I have no confidences to share and I don't weep buckets of real tears, as brides do when they go to their in-laws every year on leaving the hostel. Looking at them, something hardens within me like the solid kernel of a mango; a hard core that resists being dunked in this universal morass of sentimental confidences.

"Oh yes!" Kishwar turns around. "May I wear your new chappals now, since you're not going?"

I picked up Mother's letter again. I'd overlooked the last sentence on the outside, "Do go and look up Munna Chacha once. I hear he's not been well again. Tell him I asked after him." Huh! "Asked after him, asked after him," I pull a horrid face. Am I the only one left to oblige various households and to make their members beholden to my esteemed Ma? Go and visit them and you're stuck for hours in their living rooms, where the likes of Munna Chacha inform you seriously that when Mars will enter the orbit of Venus then his chronic stomach ailment will be cured and also that when the moon will be eclipsed by Rahu this coming month, then his phlegm and bile will start acting up.

Crash! The door shot open like in the movies. Enter Pushy. She'd kicked the door open because her hands were not free. She tossed several packages at me, entirely ignoring my heart-rending screams.

"Oy Dummy, see what we picked up!" We get busy looking at her shopping. Pushy is one of those boisterous people for whom there are only two colors in life: black and white. And in either case, she has very clear opinions on them. No traces of vacillation whether the subject is her boyfriend or a badly stitched blouse. Today she was gaga over her new chappals. She'd wear them, curl her toes, turn her ankles around and was going utterly crazy over her feet. Her boyfriend had once praised them. Ever since then she took care of them and guarded them like her chastity. People become somehow transparent and pure like sleeping children in such moments of extreme narcissism. I'm always attracted to the sight of a mid-

dle-aged woman combing her long hair, children playing mar-
bles, and men watching themselves in the paan-shop mirror
while lighting their cigarettes; they reflect such honest intro-
verted concentration.

Pushy's train was leaving tonight, and what made it *sooo*
special was the fact that her boyfriend was also traveling on the
same train.

"Does the train go to his city at all?" It was Kishwar leaning
against the door again, picking her teeth with the comb. Pushy
roared with laughter.

"Of course not. But he'll take a connecting train from Agra.
It'll make a difference of only a few hours."

"Take him home, na!" Kishwar said laughing. "Tell Papa,
see I got you a present. He'll liven up your life in that godforsaken place." Pushy's father had a huge farm in the Terai region
in the foothills of the Himalayas. Her people were simply rolling
in money, but one gathered from Pushy that they were quite
different from the urban anglicized rich; their world was one of
primeval animal physicality and machismo. Every now and
again, her father and uncle would beat up some hapless em-
ployee or molest someone's wife. In the absolute solitude of the
Terai, cut off from the rest of the world, they had to spend at
least six months of the year amongst wild animals and tribals
from the foothills. They had two unerring means of gratification: foreign liquor and local women. Whenever the men were
overtaken by this Dionysiac Debauchery, Pushy's mother would
shift to her townhouse and busy herself arranging a path from
Japji Saheb or get the carpets cleaned or something. She would
return when the phase was over. "A woman is like a shoe in our
house, but a shoe with some polish—polish," Pushy would
laugh uproariously. Everybody knew that ultimately she would
never marry her boyfriend because he was a bania by caste and
not very prosperous. But Pushy obviously did not suffer any
agonies over this. She had quite naturally accepted her fate of
an ornate shoe to be given in marriage to a man similar to her
father and uncle, and now she was happily recounting how,

after every such binge, her father would order new gold ornaments and clothes for her mother. No sir! The dignity of the
women of the family had to be kept intact, and no mistress
could even hope to gain even an inch of that glory. As she said
this, Pushy's face glowed like Ma's and suddenly I found myself
overtaken with a desire to see her leave my room immediately.

After Pushy went, a mingled smell of sweat and Christian
Dior (uncle in New York, uncle in New York) lingered in the
room. The blood-thick March wind was straining at the door,
scratching like a lost dog.

All right: Where do you think all of this began? I mean if you
really try to think.

"He's come," Babu's voice. "He's come?" Ma suppresses a
delicate yawn as she puts her romantic novel aside. Bhaiya
enters. Chhota and I are playing a game of chess. We freeze,
apprehending trouble. Some fool drops something in the
kitchen. Clang! "Is this any way to behave?" Babu's sharp voice.
"Will you eat or have you . . ." Ma's tone is one-fourth martyrdom, one-fourth apathy and one-half open accusation. Tension.
Barbs. Hidden currents of violence.

"Everybody comes to congratulate you and no trace of you
all day! The house is a . . . ho-ho . . . hotel for you?" Babu
chokes on his anger. Chhota is about to laugh. I pinch him hard.

"I got held up." Bhaiya sinks into a chair quite uncon-
cerned, and picks up a magazine. Bravo. I told you, didn't I,
that we're a marvelously theatrical family? Every gesture unerr-
ingly finds its mark.

"Eat something at least, your favorite . . ." Ma rises.

"I've said, no."

Fiery looks, unspoken anger on both sides. Ma and Babu
depart backstage. Tick tick tick; fear ticks like a clock in the
center of my navel. Tick tick tick, Dear Viewers. "Do you have
an Inland letter form?" Rude return to reality. Suruchi has
arrived cat-footed and is standing at the door. I jump up, genuinely startled (I swear). But then the thespian within takes over

again. Clutching my chest I double over: "You do frighten a poor ol' thing like me. Suppose my poor li'l heart had failed. . . ." Suruchi goes out laughing with the Inland. I drag my feet towards the office to sign the register. I think I'll go to Munna Chacha's. Let's gather some info about whether planetary conjunctions indicate a strike before the exams or not. If not, then issue the Toynbee next week. Last year, when Venus or Saturn had entered Capricorn, there had been a lathi charge by police in the university.

"Houses of lawyers exude something lawyer-like," Bhaiya had once said. "Houses of the Ignorant, Ignorance"—this was Chhota and we had laughed long and hard. Munna Chacha was fraternally related to Babu in some roundabout way and was registered as my local guardian in the hostel records. He had some ancestral property in our town because of which he often landed up there. His arrival signaled the transformation of our house into the abode of Bhrigu, the astrologer sage. Endless rounds of tea. Horoscopes spread out everywhere. Politics and prediction fell thick and fast in a dazzling display. Merriment; mirthful digs; rumors. Outside, the dogs, tied and confined, would growl angrily in the darkness: Who is it? Who is it? Who is it? A star ascends. A star descends. Again and yet again, my peninsula rotates on the same axis. Morning and evening. Morning and evening.

The birds are going crazy. Khaunri, the bitch, lies sprawled in the sun . . . "Just look at her nipples. She's delivered seven puppies behind the cooler." The flock of maidservants goes giggling past. Grow! Snap! I want to wring their little necks, kill these birds, this bitch also. . . .

"What effect will my words have on them? Rahu's shadow is falling across their lunar house, you see. . . ." Ma is discussing us with her sisters; she takes off her glasses and strokes her closed eyes with fine dramatic effect. Have you ever felt sorry for a pair of hands? Our neighbors' cat grins from behind the flowers upon the pumpkin vine. Perhaps like the Cheshire cat, soon only her grin will remain upon the wall.

Ma's blouse has a half-moon of sweat under her arms. Her temples are graying slightly. Malini Mausi tells her that she is perhaps a little too attached to her children. She herself does Yogic exercises every morning to reduce her earthly attachments and belly. Has dry toast and black coffee for breakfast for a week. During that week she wears out her husband, children and servants by constantly snapping at them. Then one day she says, "To hell with it," and goes back to gorging herself on stuffed parathas and chocolate ice cream. She's tried her hand at everything: typing for a week, classical music for a month, painting for a year, and French for a year and a half. But the moment she takes up something she begins to feel it is worthless and the apathy sets in.

The aunt's cabal sits in judgment of us. Malini Mausi looks at me meaningfully and says to Ma that there is nobody you can really claim to be your own. Shalini Mausi adds in her childish lisping way, "One shouldn't speak to one's mother like this. You are a sensible girl, aren't you?" What is it that you want? What are you all looking for? This threesome asks us again and again. Surprise, perplexity and a disappointed, grudging affection writ large on their faces. I often scan the newspapers for advertisements that offer jobs far, far away from home. I try to match their requirements, to see if I can fulfill the conditions: *Lecturer:* Respectable saris, the smell of chalk, bearded colleagues who talk a lot, drink lots of tea, sit at tables and shake their legs impatiently. *Receptionist:* A one-inch wide smile, perfumed sari held with a pin, memorized rejoinders, a way with sharp rejoinders and double-talk when business executives smelling of French after-shave come too close. *Artist:* Handspun saris in ethnic colors, quantities of kohl, silver ornaments, and men friends who laugh loudly and arrive bleary-eyed to work in the mornings. I once wished to be like Draupadi; men could come, stay and then go out of my life. There would be no recriminations, no regrets, no enmity. Whoever offered you love, you gave yourself to him. But *pappé*, this is just not possible. The men I've seen in buses, homes, trains, don't want a trust deposit, they want you as an immovable piece of property around which they can stretch a barbed wire fence and put up a signboard saying "No thoroughfare." No, no, I'll have to find another way.

I return without signing the register. Suddenly, I don't want to go to Munna Chacha's. If Ma asks I'll just make an excuse. Ha! My kick sends the pebble ricocheting like a gunshot. If nothing else, one can at least become an indecent sort of object of wonder. It's difficult, I grant you, but other solutions are no better. Period.

Kishwar is going out, all dressed up, with five or six others. "You can still come if you want." I shake my head. She goes off, wearing my chappals. Flap. Flap.

Tong! The bell tolls something. Time? Fear? A pair of pigeons flap their wings and take flight. Chaff. Dust. Chaff. I find I am holding on to my own hand tight. The dust suddenly thickens, till it's almost difficult to breathe. Something white, vice-like, tightens over my heart. The color of fear is white, not black. The hostel superintendent Leela Mitra has sent for me. She is my well-wisher. I have many well-wishers. But people are now losing faith in me. Dear Brothers and Sisters, I tell you, believe me, I'm not worthy of all this. The rest, of course, is up to you . . . but don't say I didn't warn you.

"How's the preparation work for your exams going?" Leela Mitra asks. I wonder if am being accused of something. Leela Mitra, dear, do you know your face is adorned with a moustache? Long enough for you to try to suck it occasionally. "Don't laugh," Leela Mitra's voice is a pointed red pencil. "Answer me. Do you intend to do better this year or is it to be like last year?"

That's none of your business, I want to say. Am I a bloody human being or a telephone directory? Huh? You open a page and you can get the address and number immediately. Why? Give me one good reason.

"We had such great expectations of you," Leela Mitra's

moustachioed voice becomes emotional. "When you came to the university, we would all point to you and say that this girl will go far. You did well too, initially, but last year was terrible. I got such a shock I can't tell you." Leela Mitra's square face trembles with Professorial Disappointment. But my stony heart does not stir. *React!* Oh foolish heart of mine.

"Are you keeping well?" If their voices soften suddenly in the middle of an interrogation, the danger indicator in me goes mad and shouts, Caution: watch out, girl, they're watching you.

"Do you write home regularly?"

"Yes."

"Your mother is well?"

"Yes."

"Remember me to her. Such a nice lady . . . such . . ." My mind has already disconnected. Leela Mitra's bright, friendly voice is left picking luminaries from my family background. Even after such a Grand Betrayal by your own, do you look for happiness in the family, Leela Mitra? Forgetting that your folks didn't agree to you marrying your lover because he was from a different caste. And when they departed from center stage, you had been overtaken by menopause and a menopausal moustache on your upper lip, and he had lost all his hair. Though your friends swore by your true and unchanging love. But tell me the truth. Can it be the same at this age? I mean, really? Can it?

The platform was very crowded: vacation time. The air was stale and hot. I sat next to the window after settling my luggage. A rattling bookcart came up—English Magazine? New Magazine? Mills and Boon? Perry Mason!

"Here, Baby, new Caravan," the vendor's excited hands tremble as he riffles through the pile of magazines. They are wrinkled hands; his torn shirt cuffs are crudely darned and his nails are cut unevenly. Feeling lachrymose, I buy a couple of Mills and Boon romances for Ma, and two gory thrillers for Chotka, which all of us will ultimately read with relish after feigning indifference. I told you, as a family, we're a pretty theatrical lot. We all know we have this penchant for drama. All, that is, expect our mother. Not that she's not dramatic. She is. And perhaps ten degrees more than all of us. But she is one of those naturals, who are untainted by artifice. She has none of our moments of embarrassed self-appraisal. Her unshakable belief in herself, and her values, takes my breath away sometimes. She's been serving the sentence of marriage to Babu for twenty-five years now, and despite World Wars, Epidemics, General Elections and Pregnancies, she has remained devoted to Meals, Clothes and Children, year after year. Every winter she makes gajar ka halwa, pani pickle and every summer, raw mango panna and sweet lime. She remembers the ceremonial clothes and the designs of the gold jewelry exchanged at weddings. She has on her fingertips the dates of all wedding and birth anniversaries in the home. You ask her for the year of a particular election and she'll immediately calculate so-and-so's eldest or the other's middle child's birthday which fell that year and add and subtract and tell you the correct date. You ask her the names of the parties who contested the election and she'll draw a blank; but she can fill you in on all the details of that particular baby's weight and any complications that may have arisen at the time of its delivery, with the speed and accuracy of a computer. Her world stretches from husband to children, and in the middle of it she sits enthroned like a benign Buddha. Within the charmed circle we all dance to her tune like monkeys on a rope. Or rather, we used to, because since the day we became aware of this, things have not been the same. Today, in spite of Munna Chacha's proffered assistance to Ma, my brothers and I remain strange planetary configurations to her, ominous like stars off their orbits. But, in spite of all this, for some reason my legs still tremble in a lonely train compartment and something sticks in my throat as I see the overflowing, laughing, moving crowds on the platform. I know by now, looking at those young beauties and broad-chested young men strutting about, that my brain is superior to theirs; that after they have become procreating couples who hate each other's very shadows, my heart will be a free, wild hare sniffing fresh pastures. But by then they'll have countless things to their names: their parties, their homes, their flower vases, their polished brass Buddhas and their regularly dusted copies of Penguin Modern Poets. Their bright kids will come home with bright report cards, to clean homes, and when they feel tired they'll cast off their worries with a spoonful of chyawanprash and a cup of milk like my mother does, and sink into satisfied slumber. And all the while I, in a second-class sleeper, will be approaching middle age, my graying head on the cold, black bars, dissatisfied, obstinate, sleepless, lonely, compassionless and bitter. The iron will always feel cold and hard to my honest fingers and my fingers shall remain warm and soft. But enough! No more. As king someone says to an aging fool: "that way madness lies. . . ."

"Can I come in?" the good-natured voice asks with Ma-like unassailable innocence. I shrink and make room. Holdall, baskets, suitcase, attache case, thermos flasks, clay pots, (Are-re, careful!) and children tumble in confusedly. "Oh, it's really hot, no?" The voice combats the noisy, whirring fan. The train rattles and lurches forward. Awful retorts flutter in my head. I watch her silently as she struggles with the fan. She can't straighten it. It continues to spit hot breezes in every direction but our own. Perhaps I should help, but on such socially productive occasions I suddenly grow cold. I know; I know that it is wrong and dangerously antisocial and I also know that if Ma had been here she'd have jerked one of her unseen ropes and I would have got up with alacrity, balancing myself in the unsteady train to set things right. But friends, it's not so easy. Since she's not here, I not only lean back, but also put my feet up. Those women who are masochistic enough to wear blue nylon saris with heavy gold embroidery and red chappals in this weather, and travel alone in a second-class sleeper with two children under five, are welcome to do so. I shall not be their savior.

She shifts the fan a little and it finally turns in our direction. The flow of air is no better, but at least the fan has moved. Her face shines with the glow of Achievement. She smiles. I also smile and pretend to be falling asleep. I don't want a show of heart-warming sisterhood! She starts to play with her younger child. Yes, I know this scene of serene domesticity should have evoked a response from somebody with my upbringing, but . . .

"Where are you going?" she asks. Her face is still bathed in the glow of maternal love. I name the place. "Oh! Then we shall be getting off before you," she informs me without my asking. In the same breath she asks me whether I study here and upon being told yes, I do, she says that her husband is also posted here and how surprising! We've never seen you until now! As if my very existence is in doubt until they've seen and therefore legitimized me. Bloody egoists. But my corner is so comfortable and I'm so sleepy that I can't bring myself to feel properly irritated. Now she's asking about a particularly dull girl, Prabha, who lives in our hostel. "Do you know her?"

"Yes, of course I know her," I say enchanted with my eloquence. Suddenly, a desire to tell a resounding, dramatic lie spreads like an eagle's wings inside me. "Ah! Prabha! She's a real close friend," I say, "and such a bright student at that!" "Yes?" Her voice is doubtful but pleased. Prabha's match is fixed with her husband's cousin, her devar, you see!

"I had heard she's quite good looking, but brilliant? . . ."

"Oh, come come, who doesn't know this?" My eloquence is running away with me. I launch into an exhaustive explanation about there being two types of students: one, the mugging parrots who can be found with their noses buried in tomes all the time and who thereby ruin their good looks. They look like this during exams. I put on a face like a shriveled Dusseri mango and cross my eyes. My audience laughs delightedly. "You do such an interesting caricature!" By now I'm drunk on my silver tongued loquacity. Then there are those, I go on, who study for a scant two months before exams and then freak out.

Now Prabha is really special; she's neither a mugpot nor a laggard! And then she is such a steady girl. Not a touch of giddiness in her. As I add that extra touch of domestic sentimentality I hear myself speaking in Ma's voice. Things are getting interesting and I'm wide awake now! "Yes, that is the important thing," she says, and tells me how she worries about getting a girl—for her brother-in-law—who has been educated in a big city, because she might turn out to be too 'fast' you see.

Wonderful! You have discovered the precise chink in the armor of the customer. Ha ha ha, my insides shake with silent laughter. When I tell Bhaiya and Chhota at home that I have just arranged a match on the train, they will simply die laughing. I mean, me as a Matrimonial Coordinator! And that too for Prabha Rani, who is forever cleaning her pen on the end of her dupatta and interrupting the lecture with an adenoidal "Whad Sir? Couldn't follow."

Then she decides to give me a lot of golden details about her devar: how many offers of marriage he has had, etc. Apparently the Modinagar people dropped hints to the effect that they would give him a whole sugar mill as dowry, as there's nobody else in their family who is worthy of it. But the devar had only one *kandison* (condition): that the girl should be fair, and educated in an English-medium school. So, in spite of the dowry, "we did not say yes to them." Of course! Her devar is really such an A-one fellow. He knows so much about household affairs that even you and I wouldn't know the things he knows. He had gone to Japan for a month on company work (and of course at company expense!) and he brought back a blender, a complete set of dinner plates made of plastic, a television, dozens of Woolley georgette saris for the sisters-in-law, and oh, so many scents and lipsticks for the nieces! "Now tell me, who gives so much respect to elders these days?"

"You are absolutely right, nobody does." I nod seriously, and put on the light.

"And don't imagine he cannot discriminate between what is good for him and what is not," she tells me. "He says after marriage, he will not let the girl work outside the house at all. No sooner does the girl step out of the house, then she is ruined. I'm talking of the ones who work, not the ones who are studying," she soothes me as an afterthought. And displaying an amazing dexterity in the unsteady train she mixes water and powdered milk and stuffs the bottle into the younger child's mouth. "Drink it up fast. The station will come in fifteen minutes." The train really does slow down and I find I am helping her gather her children, baskets, milk bottles, spoons, and steel tumblers. "OK, Namaste. Time passed quite well, no?" I pat her child on the cheek. I don't reply. Somebody has come to receive her, she departs.

Before the train starts two Punjabi women with rolls of yeasty fat held together by muslin dupattas push their way in, panting, and sink into the seats. Attache cases with cloth covers, bulging fat holdalls, a brass tiffin box with a spoon the size of a small spade on top. "Ya Rabba! Tu hi palanhaar!" one of them mutters. The other belches loudly and calls out "Om! Om!" several times. "You shouldn't have made me eat so many parathas," she tells her companion, "my baigola is acting up." I am reminded of my grandmother who also suffers from such mysterious ailments: a rising baigola, a throbbing chilak pain, a hammering heart, etc. These strange ailments of hers had equally mystifying remedies—making a prematurely born child walk nimbly across your back, licking a bit of lime pickle made from lemons which grow in the eighth month of the lunar calendar, eating fresh radishes without brushing your teeth first thing in the morning. Such ailments and their remedies make you want to believe in parapsychological forces and U.F.Os. . . . What? They seem to be asking me something. Perhaps they wish to know how far I am going. But I'm a deaf mute. Damning me with their eyes they once again become absorbed in each other. One of them begins to chant her evening prayer

> *Taar Maata Tarini, Sab Dukh Nivarni*
> *Pehli Sangya Tarini, Taar Maata Tarini*
> (Deliver us from sorrow, O mother of the evening . . .)

I fall asleep.

There was a time when we used to write home a week in advance about the date of our arrival and the exact time of the train, just as, once upon a time, there was a golden age when people did not even bolt their doors or lock their belongings. Then slowly the proverbial wheel of time turned and people began to lock their houses and boxes and bolt their doors; and we stopped mentioning personal matters in our letters.

"Those were the days then and this is how things are now," Babu sighs for effect. K. Chacha immediately lets slip something appropriate as he sits there holding his cup of tea. He has just returned from a month-long trip undertaken to recharge his internal batteries at the posh ashram of his Guru. He is glowing with the deep strength of his spirituality like a radium wristwatch. "If you have Inner Peace then the strife without does not disturb you." One can almost see a lotus emerging from his navel and on that lotus sits his Guruji. Guruji's ashram had bountiful cows with heavy udders and calves, fruits of the loins of an Australian bull. We all know how the official permission to import that bull was granted to Guruji on the proverbial silver salver because of K. Chacha's official powers. "Two of my German tractors are lying at the Bombay yard," Guruji had said with a childlike laugh. "Your worthless government is raising objection after objection. I have paid in foreign exchange long before—look, I have a receipt." He pulled out a receipt from a crocodile-skin wallet. "Thy will be done," said K. Chacha, and it was done. "So you got me? Cultivate your inner world." K. Chacha pulls at his imported Rothmans and turns to Bhaiya solemnly. "And hand over the outside world to the likes of you all, what?" Bhaiya asks, rising. The house crackles with tension suddenly. "Don't let it bother you Bhabhi," K. Chacha soothes a thoroughly embarrassed Ma, "I don't take their comments in the wrong spirit—it's their age . . . even when I was their age . . ." I can visualize you very well Chacha, with oil-slicked hair and wearing a godawful sweater chosen by your battleaxe of a mother, looking an absolute lalloo. What else? But he is holding forth: "Guruji says that man should satisfy all his desires, so that the body's demands do not obstruct the road to spiritual perfection." His discourse goes on and on, notwithstanding the fact that just last week when Munna Chacha was sitting in our living room with all his horoscopes spread out in front of him, at that time this very same gentleman was whining and asking him when the sun will enter Jupiter in his horoscope. . . . "You know, Sir, how it is in our bureaucratic ratrace, there are many who try and jack you and supercede you. . . ." K. Chacha leaves nothing to chance, though. He has been known to travel eighty kilometers when he had a raging fever, to arrange for an elephant for the wedding of his senior officer's daughter. He has been giving out of turn preference in interviews to every candidate sent him by the Minister. "But if Saturn is exerting the wrong influence, then one has to be a little careful, no? What do you say Bhai Saheb? If my Saturn had been in the ascendant, then it would have been another matter, but as it is, Mars being in the descendant, my self-confidence does take rather a drubbing," he says, shaking his head.

K. Chacha takes a smug puff; his name has made it to the Additional Secretaries panel this time. No man on earth can now shake his position. "It is just a question of getting there. But now I often feel all the charm of the Services is gone, Bhabhi. . . . Whatever you might say about the British they could judge real talent in a man. How else do you think they ruled over the country for centuries?" He blows a smoke ring. "The old officers were the real officers whether it was a matter of dressing in style, the art of conversation, or whatever. What civility, what imposing dignity they had . . . specially when you see those awful 'local' types we get now. They either cannot speak one correct sentence in English or they try to invoke fervor in the name of Mao and Che. What a deterioration of values in the Younger Generation! No political involvement at all."

"And what of those who are in prison for their political beliefs?" Bade Bhaiya's voice is a drop of sour acid in a saucepan of boiling milk. "What is your considered opinion on that?"

"Oh! Those are the Naxalites and the fascist types, whom the people of your generation lionize for no reason," K. Chacha says with a touch of asperity. Then, the thought of his Guru's injunctions and his own pride in his spirituality mellows his tones and he adds, "Yes, it's true that sometimes there are excesses committed during a police roundup. That is because the junior officers who take the orders are very small-minded (after the use of a tawdry Hindi expression he looks towards us for approbation), but if you don't get tough, you cannot govern. . . . We have yet to learn this from the British. . . ." He stretches his body luxuriously. He has returned after a long foreign trip as the head of a delegation, and the burden of his moral duties is still coursing through his veins, tiring him out. "Shaliniji, I brought your mixer this time . . . gave the customs a neat slip (pause, cooing noises). OK. I'd better take your leave now. . . ." (Everybody rises.)

"What happened? Why are you here so early? Your exams don't begin until the end of the month. Are you planning to drop them or what?" Chhota is nothing if not direct. He then picks up the suitcase and I take the bag.

"No . . . it's not that, the exams might be postponed but one can't say for sure."

"Didn't you people go on strike?" Chhota drops the suitcase in the corner with a thud. "Do you carry stones in your suitcase or what?"

"Where's everybody gone to so early in the morning?" I wipe my sweaty palms on my hips. "The house is so quiet. Where are Amma, Babu?"

"Hospital." Chhota swats an invisible fly or two with a thwack.

"What?" My mouth hangs open with surprise. Just like a country bumpkin's, as Chhota points out to me immediately. "But why have they gone there?"

"Where do sick people go? To the temple?"

His adolescent voice cracks with irritation. I suddenly notice how young and frightened his mouth looks under his slight moustache.

"But who is sick?" I ask him in a milder voice. When he was a child, if you spoke to him in a loud voice he would immediately hide his face in Ma's lap, and cry. The chicken!

"Amma is sick. Who else? She's the one who loves to nurture all those quiet ailments." He picks up a magazine and then throws it away restlessly. "If you want tea—you'll have to wait. Hari has gone to the market."

"What is the matter with her?"

"Don't know. She is supposed to have a lump in the breast. They have admitted her for a biopsy. She's been there for two days. They'll remove her stitches either today or tomorrow but she will come home today. Babu and Bhaiya have gone to get her." He then makes some more wild gestures in the air, and wrinkles his nose. "Why don't you have a wash? You smell like a goat."

I give him a dirty look and disappear into the bathroom. Trust Ma to choose the most dramatically effective time for everything. As if the uncertainty and tension of exams were not enough, we now have this. Lump in the breast indeed! My soap cake slips under the low wooden stool. Bloody Hell! I'll settle you. Gnashing my teeth I thrust my hand beneath the stool to retrieve it. The ancient wooden stool looks clean enough on top, but the continuous assault of water has turned the wood beneath into a soft and slimy pulp. As I wash the slime off my nails I promise myself that I'll kick up a fuss as soon as I get out about how the cleaning and scouring in this house is superficial, only the surfaces are cleaned, it doesn't matter to anyone what lies in the hidden nooks. Ha! I reach for my towel only to find I've left it outside. I grind my teeth and call "Chhota! Towel!" Any other time Chhota would have played pranks and after much pleading would grudgingly extend the towel towards me, only to jerk it out of reach and land it in water at the last minute. Today, however, the towel is handed over to me without a murmur.

"What was the reaction to it here?" I quiz Chhota about the union budget which the newspapers are full of, while drying my hair. "Huh!" Chhota shrugs. "Everybody knows, things will go on as before. It's just a big tamasha every time."

"Suppose there is a difference this time. Then?"

"Do you ever read the papers there?" Chhota puts a badly made cup of tea before me. "If you did, you wouldn't . . ." He breaks off in midsentence and starts scratching his back.

"No, tell me really, *if* you could cast your vote, whom would you vote for *now*? If you could vote."

"Why should I tell you?" Chhota's eyes have the familiar impish gleam for a moment, then he leans forwad confidentially. "You know everybody's lips are sealed on this issue. Even Hari, if you ask him, he'll avoid answering you."

"Meaning?"

"Meaning what? What does a vote mean anyway?" We both fall silent. What meaning does anything have anymore? Suddenly I feel that coming home for the vacation was so pointless, if you wish to consider it as a return to one's roots and all that. Well, good luck to me, I tell myself. And I have to spend *ten* days here.

I was going towards the dustbin when I heard the car stop, then doors opened and closed and then Chhota's yell: "Sudha's come, she's inside. Her college may go on strike. . . ." I was also outside by then. Amma looked the same, except that her forehead didn't have the usual vermilion mark and her hair looked a little dishevelled, making her look tired. "When did you arrive?" Amma puts her hand on my shoulder. "You could have sent a telegram, at least. How did you come from the station?"

"I knew the engine driver—he drove the train right up to our door." "This girl's cheek." Amma's voice is, as always, half full of complaint and half of laughter. Her arms encircle me briefly but I feel that she is not embracing me but the space created by me.

"When did you come?" I ask Bhaiya.

"Two, or was it three, days ago." He answers carelessly and starts unloading the luggage with Babu. The luggage, Amma, Babu and Bhaiya all suddenly seem to give off a strong hospital odor. Tired, sick somehow, extinguished. A thermos flask topples with a crash. "Has it broken?" Amma asks entering the house. "It was new . . ." Her tone is tired, but reproachful.

"Be careful, yar," Babu throws over the shoulder. Bhaiya's face tightens and the hospital odor sharpens.

"It was worth twenty-six rupees, fifty-seven paise—you understand, blockhead?" Bhaiya tells Chhota.

"And the sales tax was extra," Chhota adds. "That too, we bought it a long time ago—today it'll be . . ." Both of them start laughing.

Amma lies down in her room. "You'll have tea?" I inquire.

"No, I don't feel like it. I'll have a bath first. Then I might." Amma covers her eyes with her hands. I get up and wander outside. Unwanted and Redundant. Then I spy Chhota leafing through the books I'd brought in my bag and I launch into a quarrel immediately. "Who permitted you to riffle through my things without my permission? There's nothing private in this home. Everything is Public Property." I choke on my rage. Chhota drops the books angrily. He makes a few Judo motions in the air and goes away. Now he won't touch these books, ever, though I'd actually brought them for him.

Babu is reading the newspaper. I sit down fretfully. "What about your exams?" he asks mildly. He looks slack. His mind is always elsewhere when he's talking to me. I give a noncommittal answer and pick up a magazine and he goes back to his newspaper headlines.

"Taxes are lower this time." I suppress a yawn determinedly.

"Yes. . . . Let's see what happens." Babu seems to be reading out his words from the newspaper. Chhota enters after banging the door shut. "Yar! Try to shut the door without making such a racket." Babu shakes open the newspaper testily. In the corner of the page facing me, a model with a cauliflower-sized flower in her hair is exhorting us to buy a TV. Our town does not even have a TV substation yet. Last year a cinema hall with a 70 mm screen came up and for the locals it is still as big a wonder as the Taj Mahal.

Hai! How will these holidays ever pass, yars? I suppress another yawn. Earlier, we used to see several movies during the holidays, and after seeing one, we would come into the house enacting a new role each time. We are all born actors here. Even while drawing the curtains, raising one's eyebrows, shrugging one's shoulders, we behave as though the eyes of an invisible audience are on us. Babu did not approve of this tomfoolery of ours. His contention was that you are either successful or unsuccessful in life. There is nothing in between. Therefore we must take life seriously and cut out all such nonsense as soon as possible. But we knew that his disapproval was also as much of a pose as ours. I felt a sudden surge of affection for Babu.

"Arre, Bhai where is the patient?" My loving heart sinks to my shoes as K. Chacha materializes with a basket of fruit.

"Come, yar!" Babu puts the newspaper aside and the warning bells begin to ring inside me. I had better warn my brothers. It is Sunday today, the others will also appear soon. We've had it.

"Where is Bhabhi?" Chacha lowers his voice.

"She's asleep, I think."

"She's not sleeping, she's having a bath." Chhota's young, adolescent voice.

"Arre, Chhota, Bhai come here a minute," K. Chacha looks meaningfully at Babu. "Let us also have the pleasure of meeting our Angry Young Man. We believe some people are turning heavily Marxist these days." "Chhota . . ." Babu's commanding voice makes something stretch and snap inside me. However, there is no movement backstage, where Chhota waits in the wings.

"What an age. . . . Yar! I am an alien in my own house—these young striplings behave as if they are my uncles. There is my older Crown Prince who believes every elder is his natural enemy—we were also young men once, but we never displayed such . . ." Babu is the Wronged Suffering Father now. He only lacks a satin dressing gown and a cigarette to look like his counterpart in Hindi masala movies. What crisp dialogues, what gestures—Bravo!

I drag my feet inwards. It had all started again. I feel, I should perhaps start crying. Instead, I turn the transistor on full blast.

Morning. I gently pick up the drowsing house, scrutinize it, lob it away and catch it again. Now it lies flat on my palm, quiet and inert. Caught between the hope and anxiety of being thrown up again. I put it back and pull the sheet over my head. It's quite early still, and what should I get up for anyway?

Our town lacks late risers. Not surprising either. The streets are deserted by seven in the evening and at ten there is a hushed silence. And not only the quiet of night but high noon also induces the same soporific atmosphere. Everything flows and moves gently, like marine vegetation under seawater. This may seem like poetry to some, but it is almost maddening if you are an eighteen-year-old, and straining against the bit with the energy of a wild horse. Parents like ours, who consider themselves liberal, will say "Why don't you go out for a while?" But the question is, where? Where? Where? The height of trendiness among the town's well-heeled youth is to go to the Civil Bazar for a Softy ice cream. Once there, you sink into the unhealthy semidarkness of the restaurant with an English name, redolent with the smell of raw onions and roasted fennel seeds. The waiters with their gravy-stained jackets hover in the background, always eager to snatch the menu away from you the moment you have placed your order. The other alternative is to take the air on the promenade in front of the row of shops which sell shiny and useless plastic gadgets and flashy saris, ending at the Khadi Ashram with its year round display of dusty quilts and the chemist's shop with a neon sign! Just forget it!

The day yawned ahead and we were loath to face it. The sun was pleasant in the courtyard. Later it would be too hot. Amma asks whether we have all had breakfast properly. Reassured, she goes back to the book I had bought. When I see her reading those awful romances at her age, and with such total emotional involvement, I feel my hair turning gray like King Yayati of the Fables. "It's a good book," she smiles her approval of my taste. Oh! Great riddle of human life! And, as always, she repeats her usual question: why don't people write such romances in Hindi? It's not that we lack rich feudal families or that there is a dearth of romance in India, then. . . . Why?

I explode.

"You refuse to go anywhere, or to move with people of your own age! So what else can you do except be impertinent to your elders. Ah well! We won't be around long and we *have* to bear the punishment of being parents . . ." and she lies down. The room is full of the harsh light of midday. Bhaiya and Chhota have disappeared like magical dwarfs and who is left? Yours truly—as always.

Rring . . . the phone rings outside. I pick it up. It's Bua, asking for Amma. I tell her she's resting.

"Is she unwell?" she asks.

"Yes," I reply.

"Oh! What's wrong?" she inquires.

"Nothing much, there was a lump in her breast which was removed for a biopsy."

"Has the report come?" Her tone is moving like the jaws of a camel. Is it worry? Curiosity? Interest?

"No, not yet, it should come by tomorrow or the day after," I say.

"Imagine, we live in the same town but one doesn't get to know what's happening. It is only because I call now and then that I get news of your well-being. Nobody ever bothers from your end. I didn't even know you all had come." Silence. "OK, come over sometime. Ashish and Nisha remember you."

"Right," I answer in good-niece tones and put the phone down.

Between Bua's house and ours there stretches a long thread of civilized suspicion upon which flutter, like torn kites, many tales of disapprobation, hearsay, social obligation, and family politics. The exact balance between affection and scorn is never clear, but on social occasions the formal facade of good relations is kept up.

"Who was that on the phone?" Amma is sitting outside.

"Bua."

"Was she cross?"

"Don't know. But even if she was, what do you care?"

"Oh! You don't realize. These little things . . ." Amma's tone invites one to share a cushion-like expanse of mysterious feminine hunches. But by the time she draws a breath and begins to link all this to a deep mystic spiritualism, I have jumped clear.

"Oh, forget it, Ma. Why do you let all this bother you? You'll make yourself ill." I pick up a book.

"When do your exams start?"

"Don't know."

"You have some idea, surely?"

"I don't know, I told you. The papers have to go badly anyway, so they will." Amma starts laughing, "As if your papers have ever gone badly."

"Is there any guarantee?" Ugly creatures stir inside me again. "Or will your Munna Chacha's planets and stars defend me on this front also?"

Amma was in no mood for argument just then so she

evaded the issue. "Even if you don't believe, Munna says that during the period of Jupiter, Mahadasha, the Mind-Force is always . . ."

"Suppose, just to disprove Munna Chacha's prediction, I fail? Tell me, can you stop that?"

If Amma is not in the mood to quarrel, not even Narad Muni can incite her. She just laughs at my remarks. "Why have you been trying to pick a fight since the morning? Why don't you go out for a bit? You have so many old friends here. Get someone to drop you there."

"They are all such Prize Bores," I stretch myself like a catapult and land on the cot.

"I'll tell you Amma, you marry me off," I say very solemnly, jigging my legs. "I have only four demands. One, that the man should be very good-natured and never throw tantrums; two, he should be an only son so that there are no sisters-in-law; three, he should be reasonably good-looking; and four, he should be mentally Zero."

Bhaiya appears. "After all this education," he sneered, "all you can ask for is a tall, broad chimpanzee!"

My kick was off the mark as always. However, after a long time we all found ourselves laughing together. I happily searched for another clownish phrase but as I told you, happiness is ephemeral in this house. Just then: Ring! The bell rang. The Mausis had arrived. Laden with children, keys, baskets and commiseration. We quickly withdrew and began to plan quick disappearances.

"There seems to be a lot going on in the house today." Malini Mausi sat down. Shalini Mausi began scolding her spoilt little son in English.

"Sudha, please go and pay off the scooter wallah outside." Malini Mausi opened her purse.

"Why, what's become of the car?" Amma was fondling Shalini Mausi's daughter.

"Oh! Don't mention that wretched car. After all, it's an old one and has to be sent to the garage every week and the bill is never less than two hundred rupees. We're really in a spot with this rise in prices." Chhota and Bhaiya had ben smart and had slipped off to pay the scooter before me. I look about helplessly: Trapped.

"Shalini, has your Ayah decided whether she's staying or leaving?" No sooner had Amma asked this than Shalini Mausi's suppressed feelings spewed forth. Looking at her now one would never imagine that in her time she possessed a first-rate brain and often woke at 3 A.M. to make notes on E. M. Forster. . . . She had been rendered so timorous and soft by Malini Mausi's bitter asceticism, Munna Chacha's horoscopes, and K. Chacha's jokes, that her very spirit was weary, and Bhaiya maintains that if she hurt herself, she would bleed tears and not blood. Tch, tch, tch. . . . Even now Malini Mausi and Ma, guarding the relevance of the context, cluck consolingly like protective hens around her and grumble in English.

"Poor thing. . . . She really has a problem."

"Yes! That's true. Small children and nobody to help."

"She's had such a sheltered upbringing."

"Really, society is becoming so western, yet the housewife here has no access to any of the facilities available there."

"And the same problems to contend with; and to top it all the price rise." Quietly, I gathered up my books and was just about to make my escape, when Shalini Mausi, having finished her daily lament, and had her dose of familial sympathy, stopped me. "Where are you off to? Sit with us."

"I have to study."

"Oh come on, you don't have to study every day of your life. And we don't come every day."

"Relax. What will you get by studying all the time?" This was Malini Mausi. "Of course," Shalini Mausi's dangerously bright eyes fix themselves on something distant. Three years ago she had expressed a wish that perhaps she should complete her studies privately; but Munna Chacha's Bhrigu Samhita had revealed that her life was passing through the final stage of Saturn's malignant shadow, a most inauspicious time, during which no new project should be undertaken. Then there was also the question of her husband's convenience; the difficulty in finding a trustworthy maid for the child. K. Chacha's advice was also sought. He pronounced in solemn tones that every woman's primary duty and moral obligation was towards her husband, children and in-laws, and this should not be neglected. Such wise counsel, such excellent perception! Amma had been overwhelmed. So what if he was not married himself? Such a perfect comprehension of what is what. Leave all this aside, Shalini Mausi was told, with God's Grace you've got everything, what do you need the degree for? Just then Shalini Mausi became pregnant a second time and the matter was shelved for good.

I rise again. "Stay awhile," Malini Mausi's affection touches something inside me. "You've lost weight this time." And then the familiar query: "Are you studying too much?" And the familiar response: "No, not really." But Malini Mausi's interest has already moved elsewhere. "Really Jiji, I'm sick of my increasing weight," she says. Amma protests loyally, "No, no, that's not true . . ." By then Shalini Mausi is also reminded of her increasing girth. She then starts telling them about some supposedly wonderful slimming diets published in an English women's magazine. I stifle a yawn with some effort and ask: "Which class is Pintu in now?"

Shalini Mausi casts a melancholy glance at her son who is busy stuffing himself with sweets: "In the third." "What are your subjects, Pintu?" The moment the words are out of my mouth, their well-intentioned meaninglessness hits me. Every elder in that house must have asked every child the same question at some point in time. And every child must have hated answering it. "Tell didi. . . . She's waiting for your answer," Shalini Mausi goads him in English. She always tries to speak to her children in English as far as possible. Pintu is silent and continues to chew. In his place I would have done the same. Very Good! My Boy, so far your priorities seem to be in the best tradition!

"Is the school a good one?" I ask the mother. Before she can answer, the plate of sweets falls to the floor with a crash and shatters. Pintu stands frozen with fear. With lightning speed his mother jumps up and slaps him twice.

"You stupid ass!" "Stupid yourself!" Pintu yells back, tears running down his face; Shalini Mausi also breaks down as she screams at him, and then Amma and Malini Mausi join in with: Never mind, he's only a child; and, Don't cry *beta* we'll get you such a big plate of goodies, trying to pacify, both singularly unsuccessfully. From backstage, Chhota raises questioning eyebrows at me. In our house, scenes such as these are nothing new really, nor do they affect anybody much. If such little incidents didn't liven up their dead and passive lives, wouldn't these bored mothers go crazy?

Hari picks up the fragments of the plate, and serves a fresh plateful of sweets and savories. Shalini Mausi casts one final angry look at her children, and decides it's time to become normal again. The conversation now turns to the post-budget rise in prices: there is simply not enough money and then there is the added burden of visits by relatives and the constant stream of demands made by these private missionary schools: today it's the feast day of some saint, and the next day it's the Pope's birthday. But what can one do? The Hindi schools are such that even the principal cannot speak two correct sentences in English! There is general agreement on this; you only send your child to these schools if you wish to ruin him. If only we could send them out to a hostel. The depressing tone of these discourses disturbs our Amma's gentle heart. She then gently introduces a philosophical note: one should trust in God, no? Our lives are like cupboards, sooner or later all their shelves will be filled. Just be patient! The rest is all a web of illusion . . . your mind's ability to distinguish between Right and Wrong and the purity of your Inner Self. . . . I shut my ears and get up abruptly. "I have to study," I grumble. Bhaiya and Chhota are missing. The traitors! Ha! Life is a cupboard! Thought for the day.

K. Chacha is also in the living room. We try to block out the voices of the family in the rustle of newspapers but all three pairs of ears are cocked in that direction. The papers are full of Burning Issues: The rights of minorities, the suffering of the common people, the anguished screams of women, the call for Revolution, and editorials on Expense Allocation, Capital Investment, Budget, Budget, Budget. In the living room they are also discussing this. Amma says that Munna Chacha cannot foresee any change in the horoscope of the nation for the next two years. He can't foresee it, or is it that he does not want to foresee it? Eh! Come on—speak! As though she can hear our thoughts Amma expands: "But what alternative does the nation have?" There she stops and in a grave tone for the four thousand, five hundred and fifty-sixth time, casts the pearls of her wisdom before those who care to listen: "It is very easy to destroy things but I want to know with what these younger people replace the values they are destroying continuously? After all, we do have our culture, our traditions, our . . ."

"Now this clash between generations is like a wheel," one tired voice says. "Once begun, there is little possibility of its stopping. The question is: Has there been any progress? Not that one can see."

"No, no, not that," some Faithful for the Government of India is seriously listing glorious government statistics—the strikes which were settled amicably, the increase in the GNP, the decrease in population, the check on violence and unrest. Imagine! If such people were not around, would you ever have learned all this?

"You see Bhabhi," K. Chacha's nasal voice surfaces like the sharp fin of the killer shark—"It's a question of attitudes. Half a glass of water on the table can be called either half-full or half-empty. Actually, you see there are only a few who have your inherent capacity for Faith and Goodness, those who will say that the glass is half-full. The majority in this country will say that the glass is half-empty. . . . Well! Folks . . . you can correct me if I'm wrong." Snorts of approval spread like a stream of

honey across the room. K. Chacha pauses and then pro-
nounces: "According to my Guruji, life is like a fist."

The things one hears in this house! Life is like the magi-
cian's handkerchief here, sometimes it is a cupboard, sometimes a fist. Maybe next time it will be a coffin.

"The tighter you close it, the emptier it will be inside, and
the more you flex it open, the more it will be able to hold. What
do you say Bhabhi?" K. Chacha concludes. The conversation
now turns to the deep spiritual knowledge of his Guruji and to
Mysticism.

"Guruji has an admirable lineage, he belongs to a Royal
Family of Europe. But really one has to grant the superiority of
our Eastern Mysticism. What does the West have to offer to
such seekers of Truth? Only crass materialism. That is why
Guruji turned to India."

"That's what I always say. What does money matter? The
real thing is the peace of the inner self, no?" The discussion on
price rise is lost. In the room a deep, intense, spiritualism now
burns like an incense stick, overpowering, all-pervasive.

"Somebody says that the British are a beaten people now,
Sir! I say their days are over!" Somebody else immediately chips
in with: America is also on the verge of collapse like the Roman
Empire—it will bear the consequence of its deeds soon enough!
So also Italy! And Germany! And Japan too! "Materialism has to
lose in the final reckoning. In the end only Love and Universal
Brotherhood shall remain." K. Chacha pauses briefly to let the
full impact of the last statement sink in. "Some time ago when I
was in France, an old lady came up to me at the Louvre and said
that it is her earnest wish that if she is born again, she should be
born in India."

"If a solution to the problems of the world is to be found, it
will come from the Third World!" Babu's measured voice joins in
in English, "Ultimately, it is the developing countries that will
control the world's economy and formulate a new economic
order. Mark my words."

After this apocryphal pronouncement, a deep silence

reigns in the room for a while. Then Hari brings in some fresh and piping hot snacks and conversation resumes with vigor. "You can't possibly do away with English," Malini Mausi reiterates the notion most dear to her heart. "Today, when our only link with the new developments in knowledge is the English language, what justice would it be to cast it aside?"

"It is all this Hindi belt political propaganda," her husband repeats firmly. "May one ask in which schools the children of these so-called Hindi-lovers study?"

"And, they simply teach no manners or discipline in these Hindi Schools," Shalini Mausi says in her clipped convent English. Her son is finally asleep after two plates of pakoras, numerous pieces of mithai and four resounding slaps!

Frauds! Bade Bhaiya throws the newspaper aside furiously as Hari comes with the message that Amma is calling us into the other room for tea. "Tell her we'll have it here." Bade Bhaiya catches hold of my arm: "Stop, you cannot go there."

"Stop. This wedding cannot take place." Chhota repeats the Hindi-movie dialogue with a deadpan face.

We all burst out laughing.

Hari reiterates our refusal to heed Ma's invitation to tea to the assembled company. Suddenly, there is silence. We hold our breath, stingers in readiness, like wasps. Everything is suspended as in a film still . . . then cups clink and the conversation picks up again.

"This defiance is a mere posture, I tell you," somebody says. "It's a mindless aping of those western teenagers. There is no Indian idealism left any more, the result of this westernized education . . . we too were young once and even we studied English, but we did not forget our own culture . . . Capitalism . . . Cynicism . . . Propriety . . . an apprehension of Right and Wrong . . . Experience . . . Knowledge. . . ."

"The point is," K. Chacha clears his authoritative throat. The room, chewing upon pakoras, sweets and savories between sips of tea, awaits a great pronouncement: "The point is that today's young people are like empty vessels which make far too much noise." (Collective laughter.) "To them, it is everybody for himself. Parents, brothers, sisters can go to the devil for all they care. The Nation, Religion, Culture . . . are all meaningless for them. Well Bhai Saheb! Have I said anything wrong?" The torch is handed over to Malini Mausi's husband to carry forward. He, the professional floor crosser, is always eager to be on the right side of popular opinion.

"Oh! Absolutely! You've made a million-dollar statement. I was just recently telling Maliniji that we had better forget the idea of their being a comfort in our old age. Actually our attachment to our children is the root of all unhappiness. We suffer so much for them and tomorrow when we will need them they will have flown the coop, gone with the wind. Yar! You have been wise—no hassles for you, no marriage, wife, children. What is that saying that goes: *Na Joru Na Jata, Allah Miya se Naata.*" (No wife, no progeny, and nothing comes between you and your god.) The cups start clinking again. Crash! Something falls. Chhota has probably dropped something.

Suddenly, I realize that we have been such utter fools, complete blockheads, for having lashed out at our helpless innocent parents. The real enemy has been unmasked today. This mole who, having eluded his family responsibilities by ducking his ostrich neck in obeisance to his Guru, and carrying his suppressed desires like a deadly gun to hold up any hapless parent couple by playing on their fears with a "Do you *really* believe in your children's love for you?" Traitor! Scum! God's Hound! When seventy percent of the nation's peasantry goes hungry he, with his bureaucratic largesse, procures Australian Bulls and German Tractors for his imposter Guru! It is his trucks and berserk bulldozers which raze the slums of the poor to the ground and then send the bejeweled social workers' wives with their sunglasses to apply on the dead the gooey salve of official regrets.

He it is that breeds incompetent teachers, our crafty councillors, our power-hungry politicians and our corrupt clerks!

The phone rings.

Silence.

It rings again, twice.

Babu picks it up and speaks into it.

He puts it back.

Babu says Amma's report has arrived and everything is fine. No trace of cancer has been found in the growth. His voice is weak with relief. Silence! Then Amma laughingly begins saying how she always believed that everything would be fine because Munna Chacha had already examined her horoscope and said that nothing indicates anything inauspicious or malignant at that time.

"Hari! Bring some more tea," K. Chacha calls out. "Special tea! Make it good and strong this time OK?" The room is full of the hum of conversation again.

"*Haick*," Bhaiya springs from the chair. He is a menacing Bruce Lee aiming a Karate blow in the air at Chhota, the smuggler's, neck.

"*Hu up*," Chhota cartwheels and defends himself and aims a donkey's kick at me. He is Amitabh Bachchan, the superstar.

"Ho!" I grip him from the back. I am superwoman.

Then we all fall down on the floor writhing and twisting as though we are all mortally wounded.

Translated from the original Hindi
by Manisha Chaudhry

Lakshmi Kannan ━━ *(Tamil)*

Muniyakka

Muniyakka had mastered the art of soliloquy. She would keep muttering to herself as she walked, mutter fluently, without any hesitation. Her most meaningful conversations were the ones she had with herself, and everyone was used to the way the old woman freely held forth.

Carrying herself on thin, spindly legs that looked like a pair of drumsticks, Muniyakka was surprisingly mobile as she went about her work, shivering in the cold winter of Bangalore. Sweeping, swabbing, washing vessels, washing clothes, cleaning the courtyards in front of houses, sweeping the yards and decorating them with skillfully patterned rangolis. As she went about her work, she would continuously and tirelessly talk to herself, "argue" with her relations and enemies, and give herself suitable replies from them. Children playing on the sides of the street would laugh at her and cry out: "There goes Muniyakka, the walkie-talkie!" Adults who chanced upon her noticed her in passing, mildly amused. Muniyakka went about nonchalantly, perpetuating a habit that seemed to sustain her even as she worked.

Washing vessels in Anjaneyulu's house brought her twenty rupees. She received another thirty-five for sweeping, swabbing the floors and washing the clothes at Vasudev Chetty's. Having worked for a long period at the Rama Rao's, she now received a kind of gratuity from them and they had allowed her to build a small hut for herself in a corner of their garden. She found it quite convenient. There was a tap near the hut and a raised stone platform over a cemented surface on which she washed her own clothes as well as those of the Rao household. She put her rags out to dry on a short washing line tied to a neem and a coconut tree on either side.

After finishing her work, Muniyakka would return to the Rao bungalow. Mrs. Ratna Rao had a genial temperament and she treated Muniyakka like an old member of the family. No festivities took place in the house without her participation. Ratna Rao shared some of her free moments with the old woman, chatting about various things in a semiserious vein. Only Ratna could truly relate to Muniyakka's strange ways and she found the old woman's queer humor truly enjoyable. Every day, Muniyakka concluded her day's work with her duties in the temple close by. This gave her fifteen rupees, apart from a sense of fulfillment. At the end of the day she cleaned and washed the floor of the temple, after which she gratefully took refuge in her hut in the Rao garden. She then heaved a sigh of relief and called it a day. Lighting an earthen oil lamp and guided by its dim glow, she got a log fire crackling in a rather functional oven, and a pot to boil her broth in. After preparing the broth, she cooked some millet flour, cooked it really soft and tender, and made some curry to go with it. Then she sat down to eat.

Alone in the hut she ate, helping herself to large handfuls of the food. Scooping up the food with her palm, she swallowed morsel after morsel, freely scolding her dead husband and her absent sons. Eventually, losing the feeling that she was alone in the hut, her appetite whetted by her own anger, she ate her food ravenously. She was pleasantly suffused with the satisfaction of eating food earned through her own hard labor.

After finishing her meal, she cleaned up the hut meticulously, and with a piece of jaggery in hand, emerged to sit outside for some time. She nibbled on the jaggery lingeringly. After swallowing the last little morsel she sat back and chewed some areca nut lazily, her eyes fixed on some distant point in the darkness. In that still moment, she felt quite empty. Her mind was swept clean like the interior of the hut, purged of all disturbing thoughts and stilled to a mute point. Not a fibre of her being moved. And yet, this sense of peace never lasted long.

With the failing vision of her old eyes, she peered into the inky darkness around her. The Rao bungalow was surrounded by a large garden. Segregated on one side was a clump of coconut trees. Beyond the coconut grove was a large, sprawling jackfruit tree and nestling under the shade of this, Muniyakka's hut. Gardens and groves in Bangalore invariably howled with a strong breeze in the night. To Muniyakka's eyes, in the darkness of the night, the coconut trees seemed to sway with their "hair" loosely flying in the breeze, dancing the dance of the devil. Kokkina Halli was Muniyakka's village, a few miles away from Bangalore. The people of that village always described ghosts and devils this way, essentially in their female forms: the devil, personified as a wild, mad woman, the incisors in her row of teeth curving outside on her lips to reveal a hideous smile, as her voice cackled and echoed resoundingly in the cloud-capped night sky. Hair swaying in the breeze and over the face as the devil danced in a trance to a mad rhythm.

Outside the house and above the wall that enclosed the garden, there was a big peepul tree under the dim glow of the moon. The oily gloss of its leaves shimmered in the night light. It was a garden pampered by the care and attention of the Rao couple. It had a rich variety of plants and many flower- and fruit-bearing trees. Lush and healthy, bursting with flowers, fruits, and vegetables, it exuded a sense of luxuriant well-being, characteristic of any well-maintained garden in Bangalore. Looking at it, one could forget for a moment that elsewhere there were things like abject poverty or squalor or disease. Collectively, the trees and plants looked like children who had been brought up with care and affection. Muniyakka was very fond of the garden and lavished her affection on it. In the afternoons, she would compete with the gardener and pour bucket after bucket of water, covering the entire garden, even if the exercise threatened to break her back. For a few moments, the flowers and fruits would take on a golden hue under the Midas touch of the setting sun. Taking in the sight, Muniyakka would feel infinitely enriched, as if she had somehow inherited great wealth. And yet, when the sky darkened. . . .

She was back in her retreat again, squatting outside her hut in the darkness to look at the same swaying plants and trees in the menacing form of the devil's dance. Her heart quickened as it learned to keep pace with the devil's rhythm outside. In the turbulence of the breeze, the branches hissed like so many sinister snakes and, in the fury of the hissing, Muniyakka could completely identify herself. Her mind danced, pulsating with the rhythm of the dhvamsha of Kali.

Sounds of windows being slammed and bolted. The servants of the Rao household and the oldest daughter were securing the windows against the cold and wild breeze outside. Through the glass windows, the light of the house spread a quiet glow in the middle of the dark garden. There was peace inside. But outside, a night pitch dark. Each leaf on the trees, fanning out like the enlarged hood of a snake, sighing "shoo," "shoo," "shoo," as they together surrounded the solitary Muniyakka like a thousand hissing snakes.

Snakes and snakes and more snakes . . . everywhere a snake, hissing. If it slithers in green or brown colors in front of you, or if you find it curling down from the eaves of the ceiling, then take a sturdy bamboo pole and bring it down hard on the snake, beat it up instantly! Beat on it till it quivers in agony and is smashed into pulp. But if the same genus of serpent comes crowned with the title of Cobra and you see the proud tilt of its hood and feel the heat of its hissing breath, then reach for some milk immediately. Offer the milk most humbly to the cobra, kneel down and do your obeisance. If the same cobra does not slide or slither but is frozen in stone in the corner of a temple, or under a blackberry tree, then there is no limit to your worship.

You apply kumkum on the stone snake, dash your own forehead on the curved stone as you entreat favors and dreams that need to be fulfilled. Offer flowers to the stone snake, break coconuts and let the tender coconut water bathe the stone as you repeat your prayers, shivering and damp from your holy ablutions, your stomach caved in from a devout fast. These women, muttering their prayers, going round and round the stone snakes and the blackberry tree, round and round dizzily like fervent dervishes. Ripe berries dropping from the tree on the stone snakes below, smashing their rich pulp against the stone and dying it in vivid spots of blue and purple. The dumb mouths of the snakes carrying the sweets smeared by the women. Armies of large, black ants filing in orderly rows toward the sweets. Stones scarred with lines of kumkum, turmeric, sandalwood paste, and the smudgy sprinkling of withered petals of flowers.

It was Muniyakka's responsibility to wash the stones clean of all the stains. She doused them with buckets of water, and with a rough coir brush in her hand, fiercely scrubbed the stains away. With a broomstick held firmly in her hand, she swept away the stones of the half-eaten berries dropped by the squirrels. She cursed the women who came to worship and made such a mess at the temple. "Foolish women . . . banging their brows on the stone, begging for favors—give me a son, Lord of Snakes, Great Nagaraja! Please give me a son. . . . Idiots! I was like you when I was a young woman, bruising my brow on this stone and praying for sons. The result? Today I have three useless sons in whom I had a deep, implicit faith. I visited their homes so eagerly, but not one of them would even give me a single tepid bowl of broth. Each worthless son, lusting after his own wife. They don't need a mother any more. Shameless bastards. Naturally! They were, after all, fathered by an equally worthless man, Bairappa. That husband of mine, dying after leading a life of waste—smoking, drinking, gambling, squandering my hard-earned money. . . . Bairappa be damned!"

"So, what news, ajji? Finished your work for the day?" asked Thimmayya, the temple gardener, emerging from the bushes.

"Yes, Thimmayya, I've finished my work. But I will have to get up early tomorrow. It is the death anniversary of that worthless husband of mine, Bairappa. I will do my duty and have a small sraddha in my hut. Come tomorrow and have a special lunch. Will you come?"

"Of course, ajji, I'll certainly come," said Thimmayya with a big grin. Then he asked, "Ajji, have you bought all the things necessary for the sraddha or has anything been left out? You always take care not to leave any gaps in Bairappa's banana leaf—complete with his favorite brand of bidi, sweet buns made with jaggery, then spiced rice . . . even the toddy. Mmm . . ." Thimmayya licked his lips in candid anticipation of an appetizing meal.

Muniyakka laughed out loud. "All right then, come tomorrow. You can have everything from the bastard Bairappa's leaf." Picking up her bucket and the broomstick, she went out of the temple.

Bairappa's sraddha. It was done just the way it had been all these years. Muniyakka performed the rites that should rightfully have been performed by her sons. But they ignored the day. She kept all her husband's favorite dishes on a clean banana leaf, meant to appease his departed soul. The gleaming leaf held fish curry, tenderly cooked cabbage, sweet buns made with jaggery, spiced rice, a small bottle of toddy and a packet of his favorite brand of bidis. On this day, Muniyakka had a youthful glow on her face. Today she felt emboldened to wear a large, round kumkum on her forehead. Flowers in her hair. A clean cotton sari wrapped around her old, withered body. She briskly attended to all the rites and rituals of the sraddha, all the while scolding and cursing her husband. Ratna Rao saw the items on the banana leaf and had a good laugh. She teased Muniyakka pleasantly, her voice ringing lightly like silver bells. Muniyakka blushed at the teasing but joined Mrs. Rao in her lighthearted laughter. When she got through all the work, Muniyakka began to sweep and clean the hut and her face registered a subtle transformation: "Husband! Son! What a humbug these relationships are . . . hum!" She came out of the hut as usual and squatted outside, back resting against the wall, eyes peering into the darkness. The tree began to dance. Muniyakka enjoyed the devil's dance once more, with a vicarious pleasure. In that lonely hour she experienced her own sense of isolation with a private thrill. Felt the damp air caressing her hollow cheeks, the pleasant smell of the earth dampened by the prelude of a drizzle. Muniyakka smelled everything around her and heard the distant thunder. I won't have to water the garden tomorrow, she thought. There will be a heavy downpour. Thunder will crack the sky and rain will pour down on all the trees. And the plants. And on this hut, here. The temple. The stone snakes. Everything will be washed clean.

In the strong breeze, the branches swayed wildly. Muniyakka waited for the trees to begin the dance of the devil. Waited quietly, to participate in the dance. She sat in the darkness, a small speck, peering, watching, thinking:

> Who's a devil? And who's not a devil?
> Who am I?
> And you? Who the devil are you?
> Where am I going? And when? For what?
> And up to where?

Translated from the original Tamil
by the author

Ismat Chughtai ▰▰▰ *(Urdu)*

Tiny's Granny

God knows what her real name was. No one had ever called her by it. When she was a little snotty-nosed girl roaming about the alleys people used to call her "Bafatan's kid." Then she was "Bashira's daughter-in-law," and then "Bismillah's mother," and when Bismillah died in child birth, leaving Tiny an orphan, she became "Tiny's granny"—and she remained "Tiny's granny" to her dying day.

There was no occupation which Tiny's granny had not tried at some stage of her life. From the time she was old enough to hold her own cup she had started working at odd jobs in people's houses in return for her two meals a day and cast-off clothes. Exactly what the words "odd jobs" mean, only those know who have been kept at them at an age when they ought to have been laughing and playing with other children. Anything from the uninteresting duty of shaking the baby's rattle to massaging the master's head comes under the category of "odd jobs". As she grew older she learned to do a bit of cooking, and she spent some years of her life as a cook. But when her sight began to fail and she began to cook lizards in the lentils and knead flies into the bread, she had to retire. All she was fit for after that was gossiping and tale-bearing. But that also is a fair-paying trade. In every muhalla there is always some quarrel going on, and anyone who has the wit to carry information to the enemy camp can be sure of a hospitable reception. But it's a game that doesn't last. People began to call her a tell-tale, and when she saw that there was no future there, she took up her last and most profitable profession: she became a polished and accomplished beggar.

At mealtimes Granny would dilate her nostrils to smell what was cooking, single out the smell she liked best and be off on its track until she reached the house it was coming from.

"Lady, are you cooking aravi with the meat?" she would ask with a disinterested air.

"No, Granny. The aravi you get these days doesn't cook soft. I'm cooking potatoes with it."

"Potatoes! What a lovely smell! Bismillah's father, God rest him, used to love meat and potatoes. Every day it was the same thing: 'Let's have meat and potatoes,' and now," (she would heave a sigh), "I don't see meat and potatoes for months together." Then, suddenly getting anxious, "Lady, have you put any coriander leaf in with the meat?"

"No, Granny. All our coriander was ruined. The confounded water carrier's dog got into the garden and rolled all over it."

"That's a pity. A bit of coriander leaf in with the meat and potatoes makes all the difference. Hakimji's got any amount in his garden."

"That's no good to me, Granny. Yesterday his boy cut Shabban Mian's kite string and I told him that if he showed his face again he'd better look out for himself."

"Good heavens, I shan't say it's for you." And Granny would gather her burqa around her and be off with slippers clacking to Hakimji's. She'd get into the garden on the plea of wanting to sit in the sun, and then edge towards the coriander bed. Then she'd pluck a leaf and crush it between her finger and thumb and savor the pleasant smell and as soon as the Hakimji's daughter-in-law turned her back, Granny would make a grab. And obviously, when she had provided the coriander leaf she could hardly be refused a bite to eat.

Granny was famed throughout the muhalla for her sleight

of hand. You couldn't leave food and drink lying unwatched when Granny was about. She would pick up the children's milk and drink it straight from the pan: two swallows, and it would be gone. She'd put a little sugar in the palm of her hand and toss it straight into her mouth. Or press a lump of gur to her palate, and sit in the sun sucking it at her ease. She made good use of her waistband too. She would whip up an areca nut and tuck it in. Or stuff in a couple of chapatis, half in and half out, but with her thick kurta concealing them from view, and hobble away, groaning and grunting in her usual style. Everyone knew all about these things, but no one had the courage to say anything, firstly because her old hands were as quick as lightning, and moreover, when in a tight corner, she had no objection to swallowing whole whatever was in her mouth; and secondly, because if anyone expressed the slightest suspicion of her she made such a fuss that they soon thought better of it. She would swear her innocence by all that was sacred, and threaten to take an oath on the Holy Quran. And who would disgrace himself in the next world by directly inviting her to swear a false oath on the Quran?

Granny was not only a tale-bearer, thief, and cheat, she was also a first-rate liar. And her biggest lie was her burqa which she always wore. At one time it had had a veil, but when, one by one, the old men of the muhalla died off, or their eyesight failed, Granny said goodbye to her veil. But you never saw her without the cap of her burqa, with its fashionably serrated pattern on her head, as though it were stuck to her skull, and though she might leave it open down the front (even when she was wearing a transparent kurta with no vest underneath) it would billow out behind her like a king's robe. This burqa was not simply for keeping her head modestly covered. She put it to every possible and impossible use. It served her as bedclothes. Bundled up it became a pillow. On the rare occasions when she bathed, she used it as a towel. At the five times of prayer, it was her prayer mat. When the local dogs bared their teeth at her it became a serviceable shield for her protection: as a dog leapt at her calves it would find the voluminous folds of Granny's burqa hissing in its face. Granny was exceedingly fond of her burqa, and in her spare moments would sit and lament with the keenest regret over its advancing old age. To forestall further wear and tear, she would patch it with any scrap of cloth that came her way, and she trembled at the very thought of the day when it would be no more. Where would she get eight yards of white cloth to make another one? She would be lucky if she could get as much together for her shroud.

Granny had no permanent headquarters. Like a soldier, she was always on the march—today in someone's verandah, tomorrow in someone else's backyard. Wherever she spied a suitable site she would pitch camp, and when they turned her out, would move on. With half her burqa laid out under her, and the other half wrapped over her, she would lie down and take her ease.

But even more than she worried about her burqa, she worried about her only granddaughter, Tiny. Like a broody old hen, she always had her safe under her sheltering wing, and never let her out of her sight. But a time came when Granny could no longer get about, and when the people of the muhalla had got wise to her ways—as soon as they heard the shuffle of her slippers approaching they sounded the alert and took up positions of defense; and then all Granny's broad hints and suggestions would fall on deaf ears. So there was nothing that Granny could do except put Tiny to her ancestral trade, doing odd jobs in people's houses. She thought about it for a long time, and then got her a job at the Deputy Sahib's for her food, clothing, and one and a half rupees a month. She was never far away though, and stuck to Tiny like a shadow. The moment Tiny was out of sight she would set up a hullabaloo.

But a pair of old hands cannot wipe out what is inscribed in a person's fate. It was midday. The Deputy's wife had gone off to her brother's to discuss the possibility of marrying her son to his daughter. Granny was at the edge of the garden taking a nap under the shade of a tree. The lord and master was taking his siesta in a room enclosed by water-cooled screens. And Tiny, who was supposed to be pulling the rope of the ceiling fan, was dozing with the rope in her hand. The fan stopped moving, the lord and master woke up, his animality was aroused, and Tiny's fate was sealed.

They say that to ward off the failing powers of old age the hakims and vaids, besides all the medicines and ointments which they employ, also prescribe children's broth—well, the nine-year-old Tiny was no more than a chicken herself.

When Tiny's granny awoke from her nap, Tiny had disappeared. She searched the whole muhalla, but there was no sign of her anywhere. But when she returned tired out to her room at night, there was Tiny in a corner leaning up against the wall, staring about her with listless eyes like a wounded bird. Granny was almost too terrified to speak, but to conceal the weakness she felt she began swearing at Tiny. "You little whore, so this is where you've got to! And I've been all over the place looking for you until my poor old legs are all swollen. Just you wait till I tell the master! I'll get you thrashed within an inch of your life!"

But Tiny couldn't conceal what had happened to her for long, and when Granny found out, she beat her head and shrieked. When the woman next door was told, she clutched her head in horror. If the Deputy's son had done it, then perhaps something might have been said. But the Deputy himself—one of the leading men in the muhalla, grandfather to three grandchildren, a religious man who regularly said his five daily prayers and had only recently provided mats and water vessels to the local mosque—how could anyone raise a voice against *him?*

So Granny, who was used to being at the mercy of others, swallowed her sorrow, applied warm cloths to Tiny's back, gave her sweets to comfort her, and bore her trouble as best she might. Tiny spent a day or two in bed, and then was up and about again. And in a few days she had forgotten all about it.

Not so the gentlewomen of the muhalla. They would send for her on the quiet and ask her all about it.

"No. . . . Granny will smack me." Tiny would try to get out of it.

"Here, take these bangles. . . . Granny won't know anything about it." The eager ladies would coax her.

"What happened? How did it happen?" They would ask for all the details, and Tiny, who was too young and innocent to understand what it all meant, would tell them as well as she could, and they would cover their faces and laugh delightedly.

Tiny might forget, but Nature cannot. If you pluck a flower in the bud and make it bloom before it is ready, its petals fall and only the stump is left. Who knows how many innocent petals Tiny's face had shed? It acquired a forward, brazen look, a look older than its years. Tiny did not grow from a child into a girl, but at one leap became a woman, and not a fully fashioned woman molded by Nature's skilled and practiced hand, but one like a figure on whom some giant with feet two yards long had trodden—squat, fat, puffy, like a clay toy which the potter had knelt on before it had hardened.

When a rag is all dirty and greasy, no one minds too much if someone wipes his nose on it. The boys would pinch her playfully in the open street, and give her sweets to eat. Tiny's eyes began to dance with an evil light. . . . And now Granny no longer stuffed her with sweets: she beat her black and blue instead. But you can't shake the dust off a greasy cloth. Tiny was like a rubber ball: hit it and it bounces back at you.

Within a few years Tiny's promiscuity had made her a pest to the whole muhalla. It was rumored that the Deputy Sahib and his son had quarreled over her . . . then that Rajya the palanquin-bearer had given the Mullah a thorough thrashing . . . then that she had taken up regularly with the nephew of Siddiq the wrestler. Every day Tiny came near to losing her nose,* and there was fighting and brawling in the alleys.

The place became too hot to hold her. There was nowhere

---

*Cutting off the nose was the traditional punishment inflicted on a loose woman. In this context, it would be the act of a jealous lover, punishing her for her promiscuity.

where she could safely set foot any more. Thanks to Tiny's youthful charms and Siddiq's nephew's youthful strength, life in the muhalla became intolerable. They say that in places like Delhi and Bombay there is an abundant demand for their kind of commodity. Perhaps the two of them migrated there.

The day Tiny ran away, Granny had not the slightest suspicion of what was afoot. For several days the little wretch had been unusually quiet. She hadn't even sworn at Granny, but had spent a lot of time sitting quietly on her own, staring into space.

"Come and get your dinner, Tiny," Granny would say.

"I'm not hungry, Granny."

"Tiny, it's getting late. Go to bed."

"I don't feel sleepy, Granny."

That night she began to massage Granny's feet for her. "Granny . . . Granny, just hear me recite the subhanakallahumma and see if I've got it right." Granny heard it: Tiny had it off pat.

"All right, dear. Off you go now. It's time you were asleep." And Granny turned over and tried to sleep.

A little later she could hear Tiny moving about in the yard. "What the devil is she up to now?" she muttered. "What b— has she brought home now? Little whore! She's got to use even the backyard now!" But when she peered down into the yard, Granny was filled with awe. Tiny was saying her isha prayer. And in the morning she was gone.

People who return to our place from journeys far afield sometimes bring news of her. One says that a great lord has made her his mistress and that she is living in fine style like a lady, with a carriage and any amount of gold. Another says he has seen her in the Diamond Market.* Others say she has been seen in Faras Road* or in Sona Gachi.*

But Granny's story is that Tiny had had a sudden attack of cholera and was dead before anyone knew it.

---

*The names of prostitutes' quarters in various big Indian cities.

After her period of mourning for Tiny, Granny's mind started to wander. People passing her in the street would tease her and make jokes at her expense.

"Granny, why don't you get married?" my sister would say.

Granny would get annoyed. "Who to! Your husband?"

"Why not marry the Mullah? I tell you he's crazy about you. By God he is!"

Then the swearing would begin, and Granny's swearing was so novel and colorful that people could only stare aghast.

"*That* pimp! Just see what happens if I get hold of him! If I don't pull his beard out, you can call me what you like." But whenever she met the Mullah at the corner of the street, then, believe it or not, she would go all shy.

Apart from the urchins of the muhalla, Granny's lifelong enemies were the monkeys—"the confounded, blasted monkeys." They had been settled in the muhalla for generations and knew all about everyone who lived there. They knew that men were dangerous, and children mischievous, but that women were only afraid of them. But then Granny too had spent all her life among them. She'd got hold of some child's catapult to frighten them with, and when she wound her burqa round her head like a great turban and pounced upon them with her catapult at the ready, the monkeys really did panic for a moment before returning to their usual attitude of indifference towards her.

Day in and day out Granny and the monkeys used to fight over her bits and pieces of stale food. Whenever there was a marriage in the muhalla, or a funeral feast, or the celebrations that mark the fortieth day after childbirth, Granny would be there, gathering up the scraps left over as though she were under contract to do so. Where free food was being distributed she would contrive to come up for her share four times over. In this way she would pile up a regular stock of food, and then she would gaze at it regretfully, wishing that God had arranged her stomach like the camel's so that she could tuck away four days' supply at one go. God had ordained that her food supply should be utterly haphazard. So why had He provided her with a machine so defective for eating it that if she had more than two meals' supply at any one time, it simply couldn't cope? So what she used to do was to spread out the food to dry on bits of sacking and then put them in a pitcher. When she felt hungry she would take some out and crumble it up, add a dash of water and a pinch of chillies and salt, and there was a tasty mash all ready to eat. But during the summer and during the rains this recipe had often given her severe diarrhea. So when her bits of food got stale and began to smell she would, with the greatest reluctance, sell them to people for whatever price she could get to feed to their dogs and goats. The trouble was that generally the stomachs of the dogs and goats proved less brazen than Granny's, and people would not take her dainties as a gift, let alone buy them. All this notwithstanding that these bits and pieces were dearer to Granny than life itself, that she put up with countless kicks and curses to get them, and that to dry them in the sun meant waging holy war against the whole monkey race. She would no sooner spread them out than the news would, as though by wireless, reach the monkey tribe, and band upon band of them would come and take up their positions on the wall or frisk about on the tiles raising a din. They would pull out the straws from the thatch and chatter and scold the passersby. Granny would take the field against them. Swathing her burqa round her head and taking her catapult in her hand, she would take her stand. The battle would rage all day, Granny scaring the monkeys off again and again, and when evening came she would gather up what was left after their depredations, and cursing them from the bottom of her heart, creep exhausted into her little room to sleep.

The monkeys must have acquired a personal grudge against Granny. How else can you explain the fact that they turned their backs on everything else the world had to offer and concentrated all their attacks on Granny's scraps of food? And how else can you explain the fact that a big, rascally, red-behinded monkey ran off with her pillow, which she loved more than her life? Once Tiny had gone, this pillow was the only thing left in the world that was near and dear to her. She fussed and worried over it as much as she did over her burqa. She was forever repairing its seams with stout stitches. Time and again she would sit herself down in some secluded corner and start playing with her pillow like a little girl playing with a doll. She had none but the pillow now to tell all her troubles to and so lighten her burden. And the greater the love she felt for her pillow, the more stout stiches she would put into it to strengthen its seams.

And now see what a trick Fate played on her. She was sitting leaning against the parapet with her burqa wrapped round her, picking the lice out of her waistband, when suddenly a monkey flopped down, whipped up her pillow, and was off. You would have thought that someone had plucked Granny's heart out of her breast. She wept and screamed and carried on so much that the whole muhalla came flocking.

You know what monkeys are like. They wait until no one is looking and then run off with a glass or a katora, go and sit on the parapet, and taking it in both hands, start rubbing it against the wall. The person it belongs to stands there looking up and making coaxing noises, and holding out bread or an onion. But the monkey takes his time, and when he has had his bellyful of fun, throws the thing down and goes his own way. Granny poured out the whole contents of a pitcher, but the b— monkey had set his heart on the pillow, and that was that. She did all she could to coax him, but his heart would not melt, and he proceeded with the greatest enjoyment to peel the successive skins off like an onion—those same coverings over which Granny had pored with her weak and watering eyes, trying to hold them together with stitching. As every fresh cover came off Granny's hysterical wailing grew louder. And now the last covering was off and the monkey began bit by bit to throw down the contents . . . not cotton wadding but . . . Shabban's quilted jacket . . . Bannu the water carrier's waistcloth . . . Hasina's bodice . . . the baggy trousers belonging to little Munni's doll . . . Rahmat's little dupatta . . . and Khairati's knickers . . . Khairan's little boy's toy pistol . . . Munshiji's muffler . . . the sleeve (with cuff) of Ibrahim's shirt . . . a piece of Siddiq's loincloth . . . Amina's collyrium-bottle and Bafatan's kajal-box . . . Sakina's box of tin-sel clippings . . . the big bead from the Mullah's rosary and Baqir Mian's prayer board . . . Bismillah's dried navel-string, and the knob of turmeric in its sachet from Tiny's first birthday . . . some lucky grass and a silver ring . . . and Bashir Khan's gilt medal conferred on him by the government for having returned safe and sound from the war.

But it was not these trinkets that interested the onlookers. What they had their eyes on was the precious stock of stolen property which Granny had got together by years of raiding.

"Thief! Swindler! Old hag! Turn the old devil out! Hand her over to the police! Search her bedding: you might find a lot more stuff in it!" In short, they all came straight out with anything they felt like saying.

Granny's shrieking suddenly stopped. Her tears dried up, her head dropped, and she stood there stunned and speechless. . . . She passed that night sitting on her haunches, her hands grasping her knees, rocking backwards and for-wards, her body shaken by dry sobbing, lamenting and calling the names of now her mother and father, now her husband, now her daughter Bismillah, and her granddaughter Tiny. Every now and then, just for a moment, she would doze, then wake with a cry, as though ants were stinging an old sore. At times she would laugh and cry hysterically, at times talk to herself, then suddenly, for no reason, break into a smile. Then out of the darkness some old recollection would hurl its spear at her, and like a sick dog howling in a half human voice, she would rouse the whole muhalla with her cries. Two days passed in this way, and the people of the muhalla gradually began to feel sorry for what they had done. After all, no one had the slightest need for any of these things. They had disappeared years ago, and though there had been weeping and wailing over them at the time, they had long since been forgotten. It was just that they themselves were no millionaires, and sometimes on such occasions a mere straw weighs down upon you like a great beam. But the loss of these things had not killed them. Shabban's quilted jacket had long since lost any ability to grapple with the cold, and he couldn't stop himself growing up while he waited for it to be found. Hasina had long felt she was past the age for wearing a bodice. Of what use to Munni were her doll's baggy trousers? She had long passed the stage of playing with dolls and graduated to toy cooking pots. And none of the people of the muhalla was out for Granny's blood.

In olden days there lived a giant. This giant's life was in a big black bee. Across the seven seas in a cave there was a big chest, and in it another chest, and inside that was a little box, in which there was a big black bee. A brave prince came . . . and first he tore off one of the bee's legs, and by the power of the spell, one of the giant's legs broke. Then the prince broke another leg, and the giant's other leg broke. And then he crushed the bee, and the giant died.

Granny's life was in the pillow, and the monkey had torn the enchanted pillow with his teeth, and so thrust a red-hot iron bar into Granny's heart.

There was no sorrow in the world, no humiliation, no disgrace which Fate had not brought to Granny. When her husband died, and her bangles were broken, Granny had thought she had not many more days to live; when Bismillah was wrapped in her shroud, she had felt certain that this was the last straw on the camel's back. And when Tiny brought disgrace upon her and ran away, Granny had thought that this was the deathblow.

From the day of her birth onwards, every conceivable illness had assailed her. Smallpox had left its marks upon her face. Every year at some festival she would contract severe diarrhea.

Her fingers were worn to the bone by years of cleaning up other people's filth, and she had scoured pots and pans until her hands were all pitted and marked. Some time every year she would fall down the stairs in the dark, take to her bed for a day or two, and then start dragging herself about again. In her last birth Granny must surely have been a dog-tick; that's why she was so hard to kill. It seemed as though death always gave her a wide berth. She'd wander about with her clothes hanging in tatters, but she would never accept the clothes of anyone who had died, nor even let them come into contact with her. The dead person might have hidden death in the seams to jump out and grab the delicately nurtured Granny. Who could have imagined that in the end it would be the monkeys who would settle her account? Early in the morning, when the water carrier came with his water skin, he saw that Granny was sitting on her haunches on the stairs. Her mouth was open, and flies were crawling in the corners of her half-closed eyes. People had often seen Granny asleep just like this, and had feared she was dead. But Granny had always started up, cleared her throat and spat out the phlegm, and poured out a shower of abuse on the person who had disturbed her. But that day Granny remained sitting on her haunches on the stairs. Fixed in death, she showered continuous abuse upon the world. Her whole life through, she had never known a moment's ease, and wherever she had laid herself down there had been thorns. Granny was shrouded just as she was, squatting on her haunches. Her body had set fast, and no amount of pulling and tugging could straighten it.

On Judgment Day the trumpet sounded, and Granny woke with a start and got up coughing and clearing her throat, as though her ears had caught the sound of free food being doled out. . . . Cursing and swearing at the angels, she dragged herself somehow or other, doubled up as she was, over the Bridge of Sirat* and burst into the presence of God the All-Powerful and All-Kind . . . and God, beholding the degradation of humanity, bowed his head in shame and wept tears of blood. And

---

*In Muslim belief, a bridge thin as a hair and sharp as a sword, over which the true believer must pass to enter Paradise.

those divine tears of blood fell upon Granny's rough grave, and bright red poppies sprang up there and began to dance in the breeze.

Translated from the original Urdu
by Ralph Russell

Vishwapriya Iyengar ━━ *(English)*

Midnight Soldiers

*I had an ocean, What made of? Good lord—just an ocean! I had
a son. I had a giant . . .*
                                                        —*Frederico Garcia Lorca*

Seagulls flew in straight lines. The sky was a hot pale silver
light. Blue-green waves smashed against the deserted shore
lining the sand with fine slivers of broken shells. In the distance
black blobs were curving boat-like on the waves.

The thatched walls of her hut were slipping away at an
angle as though they no longer remembered why they had been
there. Tony slept sunk in warm noon sands. Matilda watched
the sleeping man from the corner of her eye as she unlocked a
small black tin box. She opened a cloth pouch and counted
some notes.

Tony's mouth was open, drooling, and a little vomit had
dried on his chin. Even now, vapors of arrack hung thickly in
the air. Matilda slid a tiny key behind the oblong picture of the
Ailing Madonna. Angels in lacy white gowns swirled around
her. They were telling Mary, Matilda thought, about the grand
home in heaven.

Only a scrap of lungi covered his body. In one hand he
clutched a crochet tack and his head had rolled over a bundled
net. Yesterday, five hundred net-eyes had torn. He had to mend
the net before the evening boats went out to sea. Yetta, their

baby daughter, slept in the crook of her father's arm. Tony grunted and shifted. The baby, too, moved.

Matilda ran through the burning sands, her outstretched toes, her calloused heels stamping flight. The boats were looking bigger moving towards the shore. Matilda watched, her eyes cutting the mist of distance, her palms already weighing the silver bellies of firm fish. Listening to the wind, she reined in her impatience and stood waiting, letting frothy waves wash her feet.

Sweat slipped down from her black-brown waist and clamped the red-black checks to her taut thighs. She dug her feet into the soggy earth and moved shells around with her toes. Salim, the auctioneer, was already at the shore. He folded up his lungi and lit a bidi. A mangy village dog flapped around him, licking his ankles, and more women clustered around. Bleached baskets yawned empty, and in the waiting eyes the homing boats sailed nearer. Salim threw fish bones like arrows. The drowsy dog ran and collapsed on every bone, then turned around and bared his teeth at Salim, wagging a matted tail. He was hoping that Salim would throw him some little fishes when the boats came.

The boats came in, each within a short time of the other. Matilda wandered, peering, waiting for her voice to scream numbers. To wrest in the giddy spiral of the noonday bidding. Salim stared at her with red dead-fish eyes and repeated the last bid, his smile a splinter taunting her reckless spirit. She turned away. More boats would come and then she would get fish cheap. Today she had only thirty rupees. For six months she had tried with an iron will not to borrow money from Salim. But Tony had already sunk them. Last year one whole log had to be replaced for the catamaran. It must have cost seven hundred rupees.

Tony could never repay his debts; in the end it always fell on Matilda. He did not even give her money for rice. He told her he was returning the money his father had borrowed from another moneylender, not Salim. The year of her marriage, his net had been destroyed by a trawler at sea and she had given him her gold bangle to buy another. Now they no longer spoke about their debts. His drunken brawls with moneylenders had become a daily storm that she had learned to live with.

Other fish vendors were walking, running away with baskets full of fish. With fish on their heads they forgot everything. They ran for miles, ten miles, sometimes more, to the market. Only these days fish was expensive, like everything else. It was with great restraint that she was able to put away money for the auction. Paul's medicines and magic brews for Yetta left her with very little money to invest in fish. Staring at the empty sea Matilda prayed fervently for a wonderful catch, for then the fish would be very cheap.

Sniveling and wheezing, Paul came toward her. He wrapped his long thin arms around her slender waist. Babbling warm words on her perspiring skin, he lisped that he was hungry and hesitantly asked for fifty paise. Matilda turned away from the vacant gray-green sea and tripped on her empty basket. A dark anger gripped her thoughts whenever she saw her elder son. His arms and legs were thin. His face and body swollen and bruised. The child kissed his mother's waist and left faint squiggles of green mucus, he pouted his lips and his round eyes shone in anticipation. Matilda slapped the water-bloated cheek. From the back row of huts women walked shorewards. Crows flew low and swift, heralding more boats. Salim turned to her with his red dead-fish eyes. She screamed, guttural and hysterical: "He is lying. He never buys food with the money I give him. He only buys sweets which flies eat. My son is not a fly." Salim was smoothening out the creases from the crumpled notes, the dog was licking the salt from his slippered feet and he kicked it aside, absently. She realized he had not been looking at her, nobody had; Paul was playing a game with tamarind seeds.

Paul was five years old. He had been sick a long time. Only two months ago the Sisters had told her that he had asthma and a disease in his kidneys which could not be cured. She had to wait for his death. The doctors in the big hospital in Trivandrum told her the same. Someone had said that big money, the kind that Matilda would never see in her life, might cure him. Money to buy organs from dying people. "Forget it," they said. "Try and understand, everybody has to die. Some young and some old. Heaven is, after all, a grand place with good food." Stubbornly, she refused to give in. The saints had to save her. Perhaps Tony would catch sharks—many, many sharks which would fetch a lot of money. Money to save Paul. Money to buy many, many kidneys. Carrying the grown child in her arms, she had walked for days to the other end of the coast to visit a famous shrine of the Madonna of Good Health. She prayed for three days, without stopping to eat or sleep. She would never give up hope. Only his wheezing, watery greed made her blind with anguish.

A catamaran was tossing over the banks. The tide was high and the men were pulling the boat with difficulty. They handed the basket over to Salim and Matilda ran towards him. Salim carried the basket, his eyes reflecting the diamond-grill scales of a blue-gray fish. Pulling on his bidi, a twig of ash fell on the midnight scales. Every fish was as large as a grown man's arm. Salim pressed a long fingernail into its flesh. Blood gushed out in red-hot squirts—it was very fresh. He dipped it in sea water and smeared it with sand. Matilda picked up another, she stroked the long fat creature with the palm of her hand, she moved her fingers along the stiff feathery fins. Its mouth was open and the cavity ribbed in circles of orange and red and the tough veins of old blood—black. Sometimes, on each of these big fish, she could make a profit of ten rupees, but today she could not even open the bidding.

Fathima was peering into the basket and her hands clasped a fish tightly. Matilda caught her throat and hissed: "You whore woman, leave my fish alone." Fathima slapped Matilda hard on her face, caught her hair and dragged her down. Matilda twisted Fathima's arm and the older woman shrieked in pain.

Salim threw them apart. Panting, a countdown of hurried breathing, and the bidding began. She should not have said that. Salim provoked Fathima to begin the bidding at eighty. Ridiculous. She felt her throat dry and she was shouting numbers that were meaningless. "Ninety, 100, 130." Fathima stared at her, bitterness hammering the black point of her eyes into Matilda's guilt. Salim looked at her with his red dead-fish eyes. Matilda undid the damp knot and counted thirty old notes into his outstretched hand and told him she would give him the hundred tomorrow. The weight of the fish basket on her head was her equilibrium. She felt secure and real. Women with fish were not allowed to ride in buses, so she had to walk fifteen miles to the market.

The other vendors had already reached the ferry, she must hurry. Matilda walked quickly. As she passed the sweet shop she saw Paul, his eyes fixed like a spider on the glass jar, the pink and yellow egg-sweets ballooning into a frightening fantasy. She pressed a coin into his wafer-thin palm. His smile faded into the dusty horizon of his mother's preoccupation.

From the vacant paths that narrowly slit rows of thatched huts, she could see the late noon boats breaking through the high tide and moving into the deep sea for the night fishing. Tony. Tony drunk. Tony sick and vituperative. Tony corroded with seawater. Tony with five hundred torn net-eyes. She turned back home.

The thatched walls were slipping on the sands; each time she had to bend lower to enter. The fumes of arrack were as thick as a whole distillery smashed to smithereens on one man's soul.

She held his smooth mahogany arms and shook him. Flies scattered from his sleeping face and studded the torn coconut matting like nails. His hands were thrown apart like Jesus's. She crossed her heart . . . asking forgiveness. God was no drunkard. She slapped him hard. Startled, his eyes opened like a child's into a nightmare. His lips and teeth meshed in a cobweb of stale saliva. "When will you mend your net? When will you go to sea? After all the fish have been taken by other men? After your children and woman have starved to death?"

Rubbing the stupor from his eyes, his lips warped a smile. She stared at him, enraged and humiliated. She watched him fumble, groan, twisting his perfect body into a thousand trivial distortions. When at last he was able to stand up they stared at each other with the sharp white electric flare of ritualized hatred.

The voices awoke the baby and she began to whimper. Tears moved in soft rivulets over tiny granules of gold sand that were embedded in her cheeks. She turned over on her belly and wriggled a pair of oval bottoms. She discharged a gray gruel clotted with dark blood. Matilda snatched the child away in distress and impatience wishing that there was some way of staying home, away from the market route.

Yetta had had loose motions for days. The mantravadi said a lizard was eating her stomach. She was too small for exorcism and so he had prescribed an herbal brew, but she had not grown any better. She had not taken Yetta to the doctor because she did not believe that those who had given up on Paul could save other human beings. She was also afraid of their predictions. They had told her to care more for Yetta because she would live. But she could not cut love like a fish and divide it between life and death. Matilda threw sand over the excreta and threw the congealed mass outside. She dropped the galvanized iron bucket into the cement well and yanked out the rope in rough jerky movements. Sharp metal rims scraped the mossy walls and she washed the baby in green water. Her basket of fish lay waiting on a stump. She was late for the market. Tony stood watching her and Paul sucked noisily. The egg-sweet made a lump in his bloated cheek and pink saliva dribbled from his mouth.

Covering the basket with bark, she saw that the blood had hardened where Salim had cut the fish with his nail. She began to run, wide, the tendons of her thighs stretching like blades. It was fortunate that she had not invested in sardine or mackerel of which there were quite a lot these days. There would still be a market for her big fish. She walked fast, faster. Matilda felt that dull glow of delight in an unexpected speculation. These days her spirit did not gamble. The fight with Fathima had sent the blood coursing to her brain. She had desperately wanted to sell the basket of big fish today. She was glad that Fathima had started the fight. She did not think Fathima was a whore or even that it was such a bad thing to be a whore. Fathima had helped so much at Paul's first communion. But she did not want her to take the fish today. She was glad that Fathima had helped to start the fight. Salim was a dog. A poisonous dog. She had felt violated when he had intervened. If she were not a Christian she would curse him, she still could, sometime . . . when God wasn't looking. If she had a good sale, she would buy a banana for Fathima's youngest daughter.

Tony dragged his net under the fan shadow of the solitary coconut palm and bent down to work. Between tacks he slurped arrack, throwing back his head to savor the rush of alcohol. A shield of sunlight metalled the child's bloated chest and he sucked, wheezed, sucked and wheezed. "*Aya* Paul, come here and sit next to me. You don't respect me because I drink, huh? You know why I drink, huh? I drink because there is no fish in the sea. See those trawler boats? They take away all the fish and kill the eggs. Because there is no fish for the fishermen those fellows are making arrack instead of fishing. Because they are making arrack instead of fishing, I am drinking instead of fishing. Ha, reason is smart, no?" He slapped the boy's back. "Tell your mother. She will slice your tongue into ribbons." Paul smiles. "You know why we paint our chickens pink? So that vultures don't recognize them. Poor little Paul, you are stupid. Your poor mother, she wanted you to go to school and study to become a bus driver, not some stupid fisherman. I don't care. Kaddallamma is our mother, for her any son of mine is good enough. Go to sea. The sea always has a place for us and our children."

Matilda rubbed the aching tissues of her insteps on the chips of granite that floored the black tar road. She loved to hear the big rumble that buses made and even the delicate squeal of the occasional car. They made the roads a little dirty, splashing water and dust around. Still, they were nice. Nobody moved when those came, they always stood in corners, leaning against walls, watching the huge round wheels turning. A blue bus went past and Matilda watched with a flickering pause of pleasure. Some seven months ago, when Yetta was only two months old, a social worker had come visiting the village. She was fair and pretty. She had worn a white starched sari with a thread border of mango leaves in black. She had worn black and white bangles. Tony had gone fishing when the lady visited her. Matilda was glad that Tony was away. The lady might have got upset if Tony was drunk. Yes, she was glad he was not at home. The lady spoke very softly and clearly and told her intelligent things. She told Matilda that they were all human beings who must live well and be healthy, earn cleverly, spend reasonably and save carefully. Husband and wife should not fight, they should love each other, and Matilda had agreed heartily. The lady had told her that they should have few children, two children, so that they could spend time and attention on making them as wonderful as human beings should be. The lady showed her photographs of families with only two children. They had chairs made of velvet altar cloth and big pictures of crystal bowls filled with grapes, bananas and pineapples. The girl child's long black hair was caught in blue satin ribbons and she was leaning out of a sunny window looking out at a flower and a bird. The boy's small head was heaped with thick black curls and he was wearing a watch on his smooth broad wrist. He was spinning a top. The photograph had caught the spin in a blur. The mother and father were sitting together on the beautiful chairs drinking tea together, in cups and saucers. "They don't fight," the lady told her. "They love each other." The lady's pictures aroused something reverential in Matilda's thin lactating breasts. She went to the big hospital in Trivandrum to have the operation. It wasn't an operation, it was a prayer, a dream of satin ribbons, and of drinking tea together.

She told Tony about it only after she returned from Trivandrum. His eyes contorted with pain, he spluttered for words—spraying her face with angry spittle—a mouth deformed in trying to scream wordless thoughts—about dying wombs and the barren sea mother, Kaddallamma. She could not fathom his fury. Was it rage at some unknown hands turning the secrets of his woman's womb? she asked. He stumbled upon her like a wild animal and beat her with wide palms, a possessed man keeping up the rhythm of his demon. When Matilda had been reduced to the fluid emanations of her anguish he embraced her tightly and fell asleep crying and blabbering, the heavy bones of his chin axing into her chest. The nightmare was never spoken of again.

Lush ferns unfurled in thickets along the river. Matilda stood, cooling her feet, waiting for the ferry. The hot sun draped the lean planes of her shoulder. The slap of water on spade-spooned oars grew louder and she leapt onto the boat. Matilda embraced the big curving basket and hummed a church song.

She paid the boatman and ran, counting the fish in her basket, her excited brain cutting the fish into sharp fractions. She calculated the many permutations and combinations which would determine the price of the day's fish. She prayed that the tiny trawler boat fish from Quilon or the junk fish from purse seiners in Cochin would not flood the markets today. Last Monday she had to bring back a whole basket of unsold mackerel. The baby fish from trawlers were going so cheap that she had been unable to sell her fresh, fully grown fish. The iced fish strangled her prices. Until now she had been able to keep Salim at a distance. Salim had a gang of boys who collected debts at any cost. If she was not able to return that hundred tomorrow. . . . Her stomach contracted.

When Matilda reached the market, it was already in full

swing—anticipation of Easter made transactions brisk. Playful, loud sounds curled the air. Matilda saw her treasured customer walk away in the soft pluth-pluth of rubber slippers. Today she wore a voile sari and fresh flowers. She had purchased pomfret, but had Matilda been there she would certainly have bought some big fish. Her crate stall was at its usual place—flung sideways on the garbage heap. Inside was a litter of light white kittens. Matilda lifted them out and placed them gently in a broken pitcher that lay atop the heap. She upturned her crate and placed it in the semicircle of the fish market. The women from her village had already sold three-fourths of their fish. She cursed Tony and Yetta. Two other women were selling the big fish but they only had a few pieces left. She smiled as she washed her crate. The absence of the little pools of melting ice pleased her immensely. With a long iron scythe she slashed the fish into chunks and measured them in her palm. The ache in her shoulder blades eased, the ligaments of her thigh slowly throbbed still. She joined the fray, throwing her voice in a few stray notes, and her eyes watched the slow walk of hesitant customers. She jumped onto the unaware customer with the agility of a leopard. She smiled, flashing perfect orange stained teeth, and pressed her fish upwards to sweet smelling palms. The knot of crisp rupees and new coins grew bigger. She began shouting and selling like a gypsy begins to dance.

The hunchbacked beggar came shuffling and Matilda threw a meaty piece affixed to the still glistening eye into the rattling tin. Night spread around the market square and the vendors walked away slowly. Matilda stretched her arms and arched her spine backwards. She yawned. Scarlet stains patterned her crate and one big fish lay waiting for the nocturnal customer. She peeled tapioca roots and sliced white rims into her basket. Street lights paled against the smoky darkness. Further away, in the main streets, windows lit up sibilant cloaks of intimacy. It was the hour of her loneliness. Wearily clutching the edge of her crate, Matilda lifted herself up and tossed the last fish into the basket. She smoothened the ripples of her lungi and rubbed her sweat with the frayed fabric. Her hands moved massagingly over tired thighs and she pressed the tense roundness of her hips. These days, she looked at her face in the broken jagged bit of mirror and saw age, ghost-like, beginning to weave its thumbprint in fungus silk on her skin. She placed her crate on top of the garbage heap. She gazed at the sealed velvet eyes. One pale gray kitten hung its head out of the broken crack of the earthen pitcher. Gently, Matilda lifted its infant head back into the snug circle of sleeping kittens and sighed.

She walked away from the deserted market square that was marked only by broken crates and rotting vegetables. By dawn, the lepers would have cleared even that. She walked riverwards down a long road to the ferry. Starlight splashed on the coconut palms. The lower branches of yellowed leaves crackled in the breeze and shone more silvery. If she could only cut it now it would be enough to thatch her home. The palms moved their long leaves tantalizingly in the black water. She must thatch her house soon, before the monsoons set in. She would have to pay for the leaves, pay the boy for climbing and pay for the matting. It would cost her five hundred rupees at least. Salim? No. She must not ever borrow. By the time Paul grew up, the tree in her yard would have grown tall. He would climb the tree, cut the leaves and weave thatch mats. She would teach him. Church bells echoed a dull bronze clang over the water. Paul would light the evening lamp. He would kneel before Christ and make the sign of the cross. He would say, "Our Father in Heaven . . ." He would pray for his father at sea and his mother in the market. She stepped out of the ferry thinking, believing, that God delighted in the prayers of children.

She walked slowly, almost at a leisurely pace. There was rice and perhaps she would take a small cut from the big fish and make a curry. She would dry the rest to sell another day. It had been years since the family had tasted the big fish. The sea sounded very rough, there was a strong gusty breeze and Matilda walked with the breeze bouncing her petticoat. The long road was like a tree trunk which branched into lanes that held many homes like fruit. In the darkness the most pleasing sight was the lamplight glowing through them. She turned into a side lane, walking faster, her strides growing longer, heart beating louder. . . . A withering pain wrung the empty space of her heart as her hut stood dark and silent. Church bells clanged in her skull and her mouth tasted tarnished metal. She hurled herself into the hut . . . a cry of dull remorse uncoiling from her belly. "Paul, you Satan's child, where are you? A thousand curses on your demented brain. What do you want? That your father should drown at sea and I writhe under Salim's knife and you die, eh? Do you care, child? Do you care? Then why have you left your home blind at the hour when God looks at us?" The hut was dense with the child's wheezing and he hid along the scalloped shadows. Her fingers shook as she lit the small kerosene lamp. The long paw of waxy light spread slow and quivering over a sleeping baby. Brown, pale and delicate, the child slept very peacefully in a cradle of sand, in the center of the hut. The flame flickered and climbed a wooden cross. Bloodless ivory feet crossed, a black nail running through.

Poor little Yetta, how tired she must have been to sleep such sleep. In her small hands she clutched a yellow egg-sweet. Matilda smiled at her elder son whose face was fraught with anxiety. Taking the small key from behind the picture of the Ailing Madonna she unlocked the black tin box and put the money in. His wheezing disturbed the flame. They had told her he would die soon. They had told her to care more for Yetta because she would live. She could not. She could not believe in the certitude of doctors. The saints were older than the doctors. She stroked the smooth brow of the sleeping child. It was cool, cold, the fever had left her at last.

Matilda picked up the big fish and went outside to cut a slice. She placed it on the flat granite stone and picked up her knife. Even now it etched shadowy silver squares. She pressed the knife a line away from the eye, a cool breeze wafted through the doorway . . . cold, and she crept stealthily back into the hut, sweating with ominous fear. Paul sucked and wheezed. She placed her hands over the boy's mouth and nose and bent her ears over the sleeping girl child. She listened long and hard for a sound that did not escape the stillness. She picked up the child and pressed it deep into her breast. Tiny thin arms fell softly out of the mother's embrace.

Her scream cut the silence like a sword. Women came running out of a hundred lamplit huts. They rushed towards Matilda, despair touching despair. Fathima held her.

They caught the fading embers of her cry and blew into it— a hundred pain-wrought screams. Without pattern or design they filed into rows of two in a line that grew longer as more women came rushing out of the night's immense branches. Matilda stood at the head. In one gnarled hand she held a fish, in the other, a dead child.

The women wept. The sea smashed against the shore in turgid waves. Somewhere in the depth of the ocean Kaddallamma thrashed around her rocky bed emitting a hollow roar that resounded in the women's cries. Paul wheezed, coughed, wheezed again. The sounds mixed.

The long line of midnight soldiers stood transfixed. Where would they burn this fire that always burnt them?

Glossary

agarbatti:	joss sticks
ajji:	grandmother
alta:	red color applied to the soles of the feet
amma:	mother
apurujila:	a fragrant flower
aravi:	a root vegetable
babu:	used in Bengal as a term of respect for an educated man
baigola:	wind; colic
bamin:	brahmin
bania:	caste of traders
ben:	sister
beti/beta:	daughter/son
bhabhi:	brother's wife
bhadralog:	upper middle-class Bengalis
bhairav-bhairavi	the Shiva-Shakti duo
bhaiya:	elder brother
Bhrigu Samhita:	the sage Bhrigu's opus on which the Indian system of astrology is based
bua:	father's sister
burqa:	a loose, flowing garment worn by Muslim women who observe *purdah*, completely enveloping them from head to toe
chacha:	father's younger brother

173

chaddar:	sheet
chhoti:	younger, usually sister
chilak:	sharp pain
Dadhichi:	a sage in Indian mythology who gave his bones to destroy an evil demon
darshan:	the ritual revelation of a god to worshippers
devar:	husband's younger brother
dhvamsha:	rampage of destruction
didi:	respectful form of address for an older sister
dom:	a community which traditionally disposes of dead bodies at the cremation ground
Draupadi:	common wife of the five Pandava brothers in the epic, *Mahabharata*
garba:	Gujarati folk dance
gilli-danda:	popular north Indian game played with a stick and a rounded piece of wood
goonda:	ruffian
Gopal:	another name for the god Krishna adored as the child, Gopal
hakimji:	one who practices the traditional Arab (originally Greek) system of medicine. *"Ji"* is a suffix indicative of respect
Holi:	spring festival in north India
Isha prayer:	the last of the five daily prayers according to Islam
Japji Saheb:	a part of the *Guru Granth Saheb*, the holy book of the Sikhs, written by Guru Nanak himself
jatra:	folk theater in eastern India
Kali:	goddess of power, the female counterpart of Shiva, god of destruction in the Hindu pantheon
Kaliyug:	the age of lead, basest of the ages in the Hindu cycle of time; an age of moral decay

kantha:	quilted squares of soft cotton
katora:	a small metal serving bowl
Kayastha:	community traditionally associated with the profession of writing or bookkeeping
Lakshmi:	goddess of wealth
lalloo:	fool
lathi-charge:	baton attack by the police to quell disturbances
maha dasha:	overweening influence of a specific planet
mantravadi:	witch-doctor
masala:	mixed spices; formula-based popular Hindi film (colloq.)
mashi/mausi:	mother's sister
muhalla:	a ward or quarter of a city
Narad Muni:	sage in Indian mythology known for making trouble
pagli:	mad woman
pappé (colloq.)	brother
path:	continuous chanting of holy scriptures
prasad:	foodstuff given to devotees after worship in temples
pujas:	prayer ceremonies
Rahu:	malefic star in the Indian zodiac system
raja:	king
rangoli:	decorative pattern made with finely-powdered rice on freshly swept and moistened earth at the threshold of a house
sadhu:	holy man
Sati-Savitri-Sita:	ideals of Indian womanhood drawn from characters in Hindu mythology
Shakti:	the female principle in Hindu philosophy, symbolic of power
Shivaratri:	a ritual Hindu observance for the god Shiva
sindur:	vermilion powder applied by women in

	the parting of their hair to indicate marital status
sraddha:	religious ceremonies performed to mark the death anniversary of a person
subhanakal-lahumma:	part of the words recited at each of the five times of prayer in Islam
surahi:	clay pot used for storing drinking water in the summer
tamasha:	spectacle
thread ceremony:	initiation ceremony for pre-pubescent Brahmin boys
vaid:	those who practice the ancient system of Hindu medicine
"ya Rabba tu hi palanhaar":	"Oh Lord! You are our only savior"
Yayati:	character in Indian mythology who gave his youth to his father; his hair turned gray as a result

Notes on Writers

Mahasveta Devi (b. 1926) is one of Bengal's foremost litterateurs. She was honored with the prestigious Sahitya Akademi Award in 1979. An extremely successful writer of novels and short stories, she has also been a lecturer. Through her politically committed work she seeks to expose the struggle and pain of the oppressed classes in a feudal and capitalist social order. Her contribution to various progressive political movements has been significant as she uses her pen powerfully to protest and spread political awareness in campaigning for a more just and humane society. Her technically flawless writing is considered important both for its content and literary merit.

Ila Arab Mehta (b. 1938) is professor of Gujarati at St. Xaviers College, Bombay. An award winning writer of short stories, plays, and novels, she has also written for radio and television.

Suniti Aphale (b. 1942), a prolific and well-known writer of fiction in Marati, has been translated into several regional languages. She is a scholar of *Vedant* and has also done a study on the characterization of heroines in Sanskrit drama. Her plays and talks have been broadcast over radio and television. Author of over three hundred stories, in addition to plays for adults and fiction for children, Suniti Aphale's work is rated highly by both critics and readers.

Mrinal Pande (b. 1946) is the editor of a leading Hindi women's magazine, *Vama*. Interested in different kinds of media such as radio, television, and print she has published several novels, plays, and collections of short stories. Though she has taught English at the college level for many years, she has consciously chosen to write in Hindi because she feels she can reach a wider audience, especially of women, through its medium. Her observation on her writing: "I certainly put a great deal of hard work and honesty into what goes into the creation of my writing: the blood group of my mind, my insides and my skin . . . but despite all this my work has an identity separate from myself."

Lakshmi Kannan (b. 1947) is a bilingual writer who writes both in English and in Tamil. Her fiction in Tamil is published under the pseudonym of "Kaaveri." A woman of many talents, she is a poet, novelist, critic, and translator of repute. She has also published many articles and research papers on English, American, and Indian literature. Lakshmi has taught English at the university level for over ten years and has also worked as a Tamil expert on a National Lexicon in sixteen Indian languages.

Ismat Chughtai (b. 1915), one of India's foremost Urdu writers, has published several novels and collections of short stories. She is known for her committed writing during the Freedom Movement in India when, as part of the struggle, she joined with other writers in forming the Progressive Writers Association, a radical organization of writers who used their writing to campaign for freedom and equality. Ismat Chughtai today joins in campaigns for justice and civil liberties. Her published works include *Choten, Chui Mui, Kaliyan Shaitan* (a collection of short stories), and several novels.

Vishwapriya Iyengar (b. 1958) is one of India's younger writers in English. Her interest has been in both creative writing and journalism. Her articles have appeared regularly in most national dailies and many magazines and journals. A deep-rooted concern for social and political problems informs her work.

Vishwapriya Iyengar has published several short stories and is currently compiling a collection of these for publication. She has a keen interest in theater and has also been a drama critic. She writes poetry, plays, and children's books and is currently working on a film script on child labor.

The Feminist Press at The City University of New York offers alternatives in education and in literature. Founded in 1970, this nonprofit, tax-exempt educational and publishing organization works to eliminate sexual stereotypes in books and schools and to provide literature with a broad vision of human potential.

New and Forthcoming Books

Allegra Maud Goldman, a novel by Edith Konecky. Introduction by Tillie Olsen. Afterword by Bella Brodzki. $8.95 paper.

Bamboo Shoots after the Rain: Contemporary Stories by Women Writers of Taiwan, edited by Ann C. Carver and Sung-sheng Yvonne Chang. $29.95 cloth, $12.95 paper.

A Brighter Coming Day: A Frances Ellen Watkins Harper Reader, edited by Frances Smith Foster. $29.95 cloth, $14.95 paper.

The End of This Day's Business, a novel by Katharine Burdekin. Afterword by Daphne Patai. $24.95 cloth, $8.95 paper.

How I Wrote Jubilee and Other Essays on Life and Literature, by Margaret Walker. Edited by Maryemma Graham. $29.95 cloth, $9.95 paper.

Journey toward Freedom: The Story of Sojourner Truth, by Jacqueline Bernard. Introduction by Nell Irvin Painter. $29.95 cloth, $10.95 paper.

Margret Howth: A Story of Today, a novel by Rebecca Harding Davis. Afterword by Jean Fagan Yellin. $29.95 cloth, $9.95 paper.

Now in November, a novel by Josephine W. Johnson. Afterword by Nancy Hoffman. $26.95 cloth, $8.95 paper.

On Peace, War, and Gender: A Challenge to Genetic Explanations (Genes and Gender Series), edited by Anne E. Hunter. Associate editors, Catherine M. Flamenbaum and Suzanne R. Sunday. $29.95 cloth, $12.95 paper.

Quest, a novel by Helen R. Hull. Afterword by Patricia McClelland Miller. $10.95 paper.

Trifles and A Jury of Her Peers, by Susan Glaspell. Afterword by Janet Madden-Simpson. $6.95 paper.

Women's Studies International: Nairobi and Beyond, edited by Aruna Rao. $29.95 cloth, $14.95 paper.

Women Writers of India: 600 B.C. to the Present. 2 volumes. Vol. I: 600 B.C. to the Early Twentieth Century. Vol. II: The Twentieth Century. Edited by Susie Tharu and K. Lalita. Each volume: $59.95 cloth, $29.95 paper.

Fiction Classics

Between Mothers and Daughters: Stories across a Generation, edited by Susan Koppelman. $9.95 paper.

Brown Girl, Brownstones, a novel by Paule Marshall. Afterword by Mary Helen Washington. $8.95 paper.

Call Home the Heart, a novel of the thirties, by Fielding Burke. Introduction by Alice Kessler-Harris and Paul Lauter and afterwords by Sylvia J. Cook and Anna W. Shannon. $9.95 paper.

The Changelings, a novel by Jo Sinclair. Afterwords by Nellie McKay, and Johnnetta B. Cole and Elizabeth H. Oakes; biographical note by Elisabeth Sandberg. $8.95 paper.

The Convert, a novel by Elizabeth Robins. Introduction by Jane Marcus. $8.95 paper.

Daddy Was a Number Runner, a novel by Louise Meriwether. Foreword by James Baldwin and afterword by Nellie McKay. $8.95 paper.

Daughter of Earth, a novel by Agnes Smedley. Foreword by Alice Walker. Afterword by Nancy Hoffman. $9.95 paper.

Daughter of the Hills: A Woman's Part in the Coal Miners' Struggle, a novel of the thirties, by Myra Page. Introduction by Alice Kessler-Harris and Paul Lauter and afterword by Deborah S. Rosenfelt. $8.95 paper.

The Daughters of Danaus, a novel by Mona Caird. Afterword by Margaret Morganroth Gullette. $29.95 cloth, $11.95 paper.

Doctor Zay, a novel by Elizabeth Stuart Phelps. Afterword by Michael Sartisky. $8.95 paper.

An Estate of Memory, a novel by Ilona Karmel. Afterword by Ruth K. Angress. $11.95 paper.

Guardian Angel and Other Stories, by Margery Latimer. Afterwords by Nancy Loughridge, Meridel Le Sueur, and Louis Kampf. $8.95 paper.

I Love Myself when I Am Laughing . . . and Then Again when I Am Looking Mean and Impressive: A Zora Neale Hurston Reader, edited by Alice Walker. Introduction by Mary Helen Washington. $10.95 paper.

Leaving Home, a novel by Elizabeth Janeway. New foreword by the author. Afterword by Rachel M. Brownstein, $8.95 paper.

Life in the Iron Mills and Other Stories, by Rebecca Harding Davis. Biographical interpretation by Tillie Olsen. $8.95 paper.

The Living Is Easy, a novel by Dorothy West. Afterword by Adelaide M. Cromwell. $9.95 paper.

My Mother Gets Married, a novel by Moa Martinson. Translated and introduced by Margaret S. Lacy. $9.95 paper.

Not So Quiet: Stepdaughters of War, a novel by Helen Zenna Smith. Afterword by Jane Marcus. $26.95 cloth, $9.95 paper.

The Other Woman: Stories of Two Women and a Man, edited by Susan Koppelman. $9.95 paper.

The Parish and the Hill, a novel by Mary Doyle Curran. Afterword by Anne Halley. $8.95 paper.

Reena and Other Stories, selected short stories by Paule Marshall. $8.95 paper.

Ripening: Selected Work, 2nd edition, by Meridel Le Sueur. Edited and with an introduction by Elaine Hedges. New afterword by Meridel Le Sueur. $10.95 paper.

Rope of Gold, a novel of the thirties, by Josephine Herbst. Introduction by Alice Kessler-Harris and Paul Lauter and afterword by Elinor Langer. $9.95 paper.

The Silent Partner, a novel by Elizabeth Stuart Phelps. Afterword by Mari Jo Buhle and Florence Howe. $8.95 paper.

Sister Gin, a novel by June Arnold. Afterword by Jane Marcus. $8.95 paper.

Swastika Night, a novel by Katharine Burdekin. Introduction by Daphne Patai. $8.95 paper. ($4.50 when ordered with *The End of This Day's Business*)

This Child's Gonna Live, a novel by Sarah E. Wright. Appreciation by John Oliver Killens. $9.95 paper.

The Unpossessed, a novel of the thirties, by Tess Slesinger. Introduction by Alice Kessler-Harris and Paul Lauter and afterword by Janet Sharistanian. $9.95 paper.

Weeds, a novel by Edith Summers Kelley. Afterword by Charlotte Goodman. $9.95 paper.

We That Were Young, a novel by Irene Rathbone. Introduction by Lynn Knight. Afterword by Jane Marcus. $29.95 cloth, $10.95 paper.

What Did Miss Darrington See? An Anthology of Feminist Supernatural Fiction, edited by Jessica Amanda Salmonson. $29.95 cloth, $10.95 paper.

The Wide, Wide World, a novel by Susan Warner. Afterword by Jane Tompkins. $29.95 cloth, $13.95 paper.

A Woman of Genius, a novel by Mary Austin. Afterword by Nancy Porter. $9.95 paper.

Women and Appletrees, a novel by Moa Martinson. Translated from the Swedish and with an afterword by Margaret S. Lacy. $8.95 paper.

Women Working: An Anthology of Stories and Poems, edited and with an introduction by Nancy Hoffman and Florence Howe. $9.95 paper.

The Yellow Wallpaper, by Charlotte Perkins Gilman. Afterword by Elaine Hedges. $4.50 paper.

Other Titles

Always a Sister: The Feminism of Lillian D. Wald, a biography by Doris Groshen Daniels. $24.95 cloth.

Antoinette Brown Blackwell: A Biography, by Elizabeth Cazden. $24.95 cloth, $12.95 paper.

All the Women Are White, All the Blacks Are Men, but Some of Us Are Brave: Black Women's Studies, edited by Gloria T. Hull, Patricia Bell Scott, and Barbara Smith. $13.95 paper.

Black Foremothers: Three Lives, 2nd edition, by Dorothy Sterling. $9.95 paper.

Carrie Chapman Catt: A Public Life, by Jacqueline Van Voris. $24.95 cloth.

Cassandra, by Florence Nightingale. Introduction by Myra Stark. Epilogue by Cynthia MacDonald. $4.50 paper.

Competition: A Feminist Taboo? edited by Valerie Miner and Helen E. Longino. Foreword by Nell Irvin Painter. $29.95 cloth, $12.95 paper.

Complaints and Disorders: The Sexual Politics of Sickness, by Barbara Ehrenreich and Deirdre English. $4.95 paper.

The Cross-Cultural Study of Women, edited by Margot I. Duley and Mary I. Edwards. $29.95 cloth, $14.95 paper.

A Day at a Time: The Diary Literature of American Women from 1764 to the Present, edited and with an introduction by Margo Culley. $29.95 cloth, $12.95 paper.

The Defiant Muse: French Feminist Poems from the Middle Ages to the Present, a bilingual anthology edited and with an introduction by Domna C. Stanton. $29.95 cloth, $11.95 paper.

The Defiant Muse: German Feminist Poems from the Middle Ages to the Present, a bilingual anthology edited and with an introduction by Susan L. Cocalis. $29.95 cloth, $11.95 paper.

The Defiant Muse: Hispanic Feminist Poems from the Middle Ages to the Present, a bilingual anthology edited and with an introduction by Angel Flores and Kate Flores. $29.95 cloth, $11.95 paper.

The Defiant Muse: Italian Feminist Poems from the Middle Ages to the Present, a bilingual anthology edited by Beverly Allen, Muriel Kittel, and Keala Jane Jewell, and with an introduction by Beverly Allen. $29.95 cloth, $11.95 paper.

Families in Flux (formerly *Household and Kin*), by Amy Swerdlow, Renate Bridenthal, Joan Kelly, and Phyllis Vine. $9.95 paper.

Feminist Resources for Schools and Colleges: A Guide to Curricular Materials, 3rd edition, compiled and edited by Anne Chapman. $12.95 paper.

Get Smart: A Woman's Guide to Equality on Campus, by Montana Katz and Veronica Vieland. $29.95 cloth, $9.95 paper.

Harem Years: The Memoirs of an Egyptian Feminist, 1879–1924, by Huda Shaarawi. Translated and edited by Margot Badran. $29.95 cloth, $9.95 paper.

How to Get Money for Research, by Mary Rubin and the Business and Professional Women's Foundation. Foreword by Mariam Chamberlain. $6.95 paper.

In Her Own Image: Women Working in the Arts, edited and with an introduction by Elaine Hedges and Ingrid Wendt. $9.95 paper.

Integrating Women's Studies into the Curriculum: A Guide and Bibliography, by Betty Schmitz. $9.95 paper.

Käthe Kollwitz: Woman and Artist, by Martha Kearns. $10.95 paper.

Las Mujeres: Conversations from a Hispanic Community, by Nan Elsasser, Kyle MacKenzie, and Yvonne Tixier y Vigil. $9.95 paper.

Lesbian Studies: Present and Future, edited by Margaret Cruikshank. $12.95 paper.

Library and Information Sources on Women: A Guide to Collections in the Greater New York Area, compiled by the Women's Resources Group of the Greater New York Metropolitan Area Chapter of the Association of College and Research Libraries and the Center for the Study of Women and Society of the Graduate School and University Center of The City University of New York. $12.95 paper.

Lillian D. Wald: Progressive Activist, a sourcebook edited by Clare Coss. $7.95 paper.

Lone Voyagers: Academic Women in Coeducational Universities, 1870–1937, edited by Geraldine J. Clifford. $29.95 cloth, $12.95 paper.

The Maimie Papers, edited by Ruth Rosen and Sue Davidson. Introduction by Ruth Rosen. $10.95 paper. *Special price for limited time:* $6.00.

Mother to Daughter, Daughter to Mother: A Daybook and Reader, selected and shaped by Tillie Olsen. $9.95 paper.

Moving the Mountain: Women Working for Social Change, by Ellen Cantarow with Susan Gushee O'Malley and Sharon Hartman Strom. $9.95 paper.

Portraits of Chinese Women in Revolution, by Agnes Smedley. Edited and with an introduction by Jan MacKinnon and Steve MacKinnon and an afterword by Florence Howe. $10.95 paper.

Reconstructing American Literature: Courses, Syllabi, Issues, edited by Paul Lauter. $10.95 paper.

Rights and Wrongs: Women's Struggle for Legal Equality, 2nd edition, by Susan Cary Nichols, Alice M. Price, and Rachel Rubin. $7.95 paper.

Salt of the Earth, screenplay by Michael Wilson with historical commentary by Deborah Silverton Rosenfelt. $10.95 paper.

Seeds: Supporting Women's Work in the Third World, edited by Ann Leonard. Introduction by Adrienne Germain. Afterwords by Marguerite Berger, Vina Mazumdar, Kathleen Staudt, and Aminata Traore. $29.95 cloth, $12.95 paper.

Sultana's Dream and Selections from The Secluded Ones, by Rokeya Sakhawat Hossain. Edited and translated by Roushan Jahan. Afterword by Hanna Papanek. $16.95 cloth, $6.95 paper.

These Modern Women: Autobiographical Essays from the Twenties, edited and with a revised introduction by Elaine Showalter. $8.95 paper.

Turning the World Upside Down: The Anti-Slavery Convention of American Women Held in New York City, May 9–12, 1837. Introduction by Dorothy Sterling. $2.95 paper.

Witches, Midwives, and Nurses: A History of Women Healers, by Barbara Ehrenreich and Deirdre English. $4.95 paper.

With These Hands: Women Working on the Land, edited with an introduction by Joan M. Jensen. $9.95 paper.

With Wings: An Anthology of Literature by and about Women with Disabilities, edited by Marsha Saxton and Florence Howe. $29.95 cloth, $12.95 paper.

The Woman and the Myth: Margaret Fuller's Life and Writings, by Bell Gale Chevigny. $8.95 paper.

Woman's "True" Profession: Voices from the History of Teaching, edited and with an introduction by Nancy Hoffman. $9.95 paper.

Women Activists: Challenging the Abuse of Power, by Anne Witte Garland. Introduction by Frances T. Farenthold. Foreword by Ralph Nader. $29.95 cloth, $9.95 paper.

Women Composers: The Lost Tradition Found, by Diane Peacock Jezic. $29.95 cloth, $12.95 paper.

Women Have Always Worked: A Historical Overview, by Alice Kessler-Harris. $9.95 paper.

Writing Red: An Anthology of American Women Writers, 1930–1940, edited by Charlotte Nekola and Paula Rabinowitz. Foreword by Toni Morrison. $29.95 cloth, $12.95 paper.

For a free catalog, write to The Feminist Press at The City University of New York, 311 East 94 Street, New York, NY 10128. Send individual book orders to The Talman Company, Inc., 150 Fifth Avenue, New York, NY 10011. Please include $2.00 for postage and handling for one book, $.75 for each additional.

Please contact us for current prices.